YOU ME HIM HER

Mistress Harding Erotica Book 1

Lea Mishell

YOU ME HIM HER

Mistress Harding Erotica Book 1

Lea Mishell

ISBN 978-0-578-99312-6

An Author Lea Mishell Publication

Published by Author Lea Mishell, St. Louis, MO 63116

Tweet This Book!

Please help Lea Mishell by spreading the word about this book on Twitter!

The suggested tweet for this book is:

Did you know Author Lea Mishell writes erotica??

The suggested hashtag for this book is #MistressHardingErotica.

Find out what other people are saying about the book by clicking on this link to search for this hashtag on Twitter:

#MistressHardingErotica

Also By Lea Mishell

Neva Saw It Comin'

SistaGirlz Companion Book

Livin' Just Enough

Illusions

Unexpected Detours

Clarissa's Trilogy

JaShel's Trilogy

Unforgivable

Her Ideal Husband

SistaGirlz Finale…?

"Mistress Harding Erotica book series" is my first full erotica storyline. It may branch off into another series. It may join up with my SistaGirlz series. In the meantime, I wanted to share my naughtier thoughts with the World.

Happy Reading!

PeaceLoveHappinessPolyamory,

Lm…

Contents

CONTENTS

Mistress Harding Book 1 YOU ME HIM
HER

Publisher's Note: This book is a work of
fiction. Any reference to historical events, real

people, living and dead, or to real locales are intended only to give the fiction a setting in historic reality. Other names, characters, places, business and incidents are either the product of the author's imagination or are used fictitiously, and their resemblance, if any, to real life counterparts is entirely coincidental.

Library of Congress Catalog No.: Pending
ISBN 13: 978-0-578-99312-6
Cover Design: Lea Mishell, Jennifer Patterson
Editor(s): Lea Mishell

Lea Mishell's Acknowledgements

Before all else, I must thank my Higher Power for providing me with this gift to entertain, uplift and inform others about ETHICAL loving relationships. Much love and thanks to: my mother, Margaret Ann (Rest in heaven Mama!!) for always encouraging me to follow my dreams; my children for their patience during my writing stints; major thank you to my sister Debra for introducing me to my writing with my first journal; Ms. Erina Shannon for giving me the computer on which I wrote my first published book, the ORIGINAL version of *"Livin' Just Enough"*; Jennifer Patterson for her awesome revamp of my cover; and ALL OF MY READERS because without you, I would be writing for myself!

PeaceLoveHappinessPolyamory
Lm…

BEFORE YOU READ THIS BOOK...

Hello! This is the book's Author checking to see if you've read EVERYTHING by **Author Lea Mishell**. Have you read her **SistaGirlz: an Urban Fairy Tale book series?** After (or BEFORE) you read **THIS** book, check out my **SistaGirlz**

SistaGirlz Companion Book

or

Livin Just Enough SistaGirlz Book #1 Rachael's Story (What He Did For Her Love Edition)

or

Illusions SistaGirlz Book #2 Layla's Story

or

Neva Saw It Comin' SistaGirlz Book #3 Raven & Imani's Story

or

Unexpected Detours SistaGirlz Book #4 Meeka's Story

or

Unforgivable   SistaGirlz   Book   #5 Angela's Story

or

Her Ideal Husband SistaGirlz Book #6 Nina's Story

or

JaShel's Trilogy SistaGirlz Book #7

or

Clarissa's Trilogy SistaGirlz Book #8

or

SistaGirlz Finale…? SistaGirlz Book #9

If not, no worries. This story is still great. Fuck that, it's AWESOME! And so are my **SistaGirlz**. Gotta toot my own horn, right?! Anyhoo, I didn't want you to miss ANYTHING!!

Happy Reading!!

PeaceLoveHappinessPolyamory
Lm…

Inspiration for "YOU ME HIM HER"

I began writing "YOU ME HIM HER" in 2015, shortly after discovering that I am solo polyamorous (I prefer multiple intimate relationships with various people without living with my partners or sharing our financial duties.) To be honest, I consider myself as a relationship anarchist as I do not have any set rules for my romantic relationships with the exception of honesty, transparency, non-possessiveness, and ETHICAL non-monogamy amongst us all. Unfortunately (or possibly FORTUNATELY), I found myself not only acting unethically but I had unethical partners. It would be nearly three years before I would be able to live a fully solo polyamorous existence. When I returned to my writing, I added details from my imagination as well as my own life after taking time reevaluate the decisions that lead me to discover polyamory and ethical non-monogamous romantic relationships.

Happy Reading!!!

PeaceLoveHappinessPolyamory
Lm...

Part 1…

YOU ME HIM HER…

Summer 2021

ME

"Just so you know, Cynda has been in love with me ever since junior high but she always steps back when I'm with you. She said she hated how you treated me and she was happy that I chose to do my own thing when you weren't around. Just as much of a freak as I am, Cynda and I always looked for new ways to increase our pleasure together. Seeing how much you loved me, it was *her* idea to include you," I explained.

"A threesome? With your *girlfriend*?!" you exclaimed over the phone. "FUCK NO!"

Sighing, I said, "See? I knew you would say no before I even finished explaining." Laying back on my bed, I looked up at the ceiling, rubbing myself slowly as I thought about you hovering over my face.

"What made you think I would say yes to a threesome with HER?!" you snapped. "You know how I feel about her!"

As Kitten started purring, I said, "But you're open to the idea of a threesome?"

Hesitantly, you replied, "Look, I know

you're getting bored doing the same old thing so if you want a threesome, I'll try it. Just not with THAT bitch!"

"First of all, Cynda was in my life *long* before I met you and I will not allow you to disrespect my girlfriend. Whether you stay or go, I will always love her!" I declared.

Sounding remorseful, you apologized. "I'm sorry, Baby but anyone except *her*."

"Did you already have someone in mind or do we have to go out and find someone?" I asked, accepting your apology. You knew I knew plenty of women that would be down for the cause just 'cause they love to make me happy. You didn't like that fact but it is what it is. I never stopped you from enjoying your life and once you get the idea out of your head that you can "change" me, you'll be happier with me.

"Let's find someone new. I don't want any-one with a previous connection to either of us," you explained.

That might be difficult.

"Maybe we'll find somebody on our trip to Jamaica?" I suggested as I sat up on the bed, picturing you standing before me slowly stripping out of your work clothes.

"Why do we have to travel? Can't we find someone locally?" you asked.

Smirking, I said, "Would you want to see their face again after we're done? This might be a big city but you know how small it really is!"

"Yeah, I guess you're right," you sighed. "But that's next month!"

Mentally preparing to hear your refusal of my suggestion, I stated, "If you're not ready…"

You exclaimed, "No! No! I'm… I'm ready. But if I don't like it…"

"We'll stop immediately and we won't do anything you don't want to do," I said to assure you.

"OK. I'm almost done here. Want me to come over?" you offered.

"Nah, Babe. I'm pretty wiped out. I'll see you first thing in the morning to wake you up," I said as I licked my lips.

"OK Baby. Love you!" you said before I ended the call. You hate that I never say "I love you" back but you hate it more when I say "Goodbye". Saying nothing at all was my compromise.

Cynda emerged from the bathroom. "So what did the Princess say?"

Rolling my eyes, I said, "What do you think?"

Chuckling, Cynda said, "Why am I NOT surprised?"

"Well you may be surprised to know she's down for a threesome," I said as Cynda pushed me down onto the bed.

"Is that so?" Cynda smirked. "I'll have to see that to believe it!"

Thinking to myself, I envisioned Cynda behind a camera while she filmed you, me, and the partner of your choice.

"I know what *that* look means," Cynda purred before straddling me while taking off her shirt.

"Oh, *do* you?" I replied, licking my lips as I looked my lover up and down. "Well, Baby, I'm from the Show-Me-State so you *know* whatcha gotta do!"

Giggling after she tossed her top behind her, with one hand, Cynda took off her bra to unleash her 40D's. Immediately, I sat up to get breastfed but just as quickly, Cynda pushed me back down onto the bed. Wagging a finger between us, she shook her head. As her locs swung back and forth, I allowed Cynda to have her way with me.

As each second ticked by, Cynda kept me in suspense while she slowly crawled up to kiss my lips before completely turning herself around, placing her sweet pussy just inches from my mouth.

"Life's short. Eat Dessert first!" Cynda giggled as she wiggled her hips above me.

Smirking, I took hold of Cynda's hips as my lips met with hers as I repaid her for teasing Dessert in my face.

"Oooooh Ooooo Ooooooh… Baaaby… B… B… BABY!!" Cynda moaned seductively.

Tracing my tongue along Cynda's walls, I gripped her hips as she attempted to squirm away. Sucking and licking kept my lover in constant motion but we were used to this dance and there was no way she was gonna win. Not tonight. Not while I had thoughts of you joining Cynda and me in our sexcapade. All of the energy that I had for you would not be wasted as I would see you soon. But right now, it was all about Cynda.

"DAMN BABY!! FUCK!!" Cynda screamed to the four walls around us. "Eat *all* of that Dessert, Baby!! YAAAAAS!!"

I didn't stop until an hour later when that woman passed out in my arms from screaming and squirming.

YOU

Uh oh…

You looked at the phone in confusion. Thinking you were ready to add a little excitement to the bedroom, you agreed to my invitation but now you're having second thoughts. Even you had to admit that our sex life was in a rut and you were looking forward to recapturing the spark we had when we first met but…

"Am I ready for a threesome?!" you asked yourself. "And if I don't go through with it, will I lose *you*?"

After three solid years of messing around, you got it in your head that I'm ready to settle down with you. Where you got *that* crazy ass idea, I'll never know but I let you carry on with your antics simply because they've been a benefit so far. You played the wifey role like a pro but unfortunately you're a bit prudish in the sheets. I thought the fact that you let me be the one to take your same sex virginity guaranteed I would have a natural born (and personally trained) freak on my hands but fuck me not.

"You like to compromise to avoid a fight. We're having sex but we're not married. I'm saving my *freak in the sheets* side for marriage," you told me happily. The hurt look on your face when I laughed started our first disagreement. Or it may have been what I said next.

"Oh you gonna hold out on *me*? Ya know The Kid ain't NEVA goin' on lockdown! All that phat ass pussy out there?! You can hang *that* up!!" I replied honestly.

You wouldn't take my calls. Made me break my routine just to check on you in person. Ever since you felt my Touch, you didn't let a day go by without me hearing from you whether I responded or not. An encouraging text. A humorous picture. Anything you thought would brighten my day. The last time I let you go too many days without hearing from me, I got a call from the hospital saying you're in the emergency room. I get it. You're hooked. But you're failing to realize that you're on that Love Cloud alone.

I love EVERYONE.

"If I do this, there's gotta be some conditions," you told yourself, rehearsing what you were going to say to me when you gave me your final decision. You knew I would never make you do anything you didn't want to do. "If this doesn't convince you I'm serious about you, *nothing* will."

Looking at your phone in your hand, debating whether to call me back or to surprise me by popping up on me, you stopped short when you realized that in the past three years of getting to know me, I've never brought you to my residence! I've always come to you or we would meet up at an elegant hotel suite.

"I don't know where in the hell you *live*?!" you exclaimed aloud. "FUCK!!"

Shaking your head in disbelief, you walked toward your bedroom to undress after a long day. Fighting back thoughts of what *I* could be doing, you took a hot shower, my words bouncing around in your head.

Nah, Babe. I'm pretty wiped out. I'll see you first thing in the morning to wake you up.

Curious to know the *true* reason for my exhaustion, devilishly grinning, you picked up your phone to text me: "Baby, I can't sleep."

Over an hour passed before I responded with a message that instantly made you moist.

"I'll be there shortly to put you to bed."

Smirking to yourself, you said, "Maybe… just maybe I'll finally have you all to myself.

A few more overnights. A few home cooked
meals. And all of the lovin' you can handle."

Walking over to your living room patio
window, you grinned as I pulled up behind
your car. Expectantly, you watched as I slowly
emerged from my vehicle. Just as I reached your
door, you opened it wide, greeting me with
nothing but your sparkling smile.

"Welcome home!" you smiled, holding
your arms open wide.

Chuckling, I entered your townhouse to
accept your hug, closing the door behind me.
"I see you're dressed for bed."

"And *other* things," you winked as you took
my hand to lead me to your bedroom. "But if
you're truly exhausted, can you just cuddle with
me until I fall asleep?"

"I'll see what I can do," I said, smacking you
on your bare ass as we entered your bedroom.
"Lemme take a shower right quick."

No doubt disappointed that you would have
to wait a little longer to feel my Touch, you followed me into your master bathroom. Watching as I undressed, you asked, "How was your
day, Baby?"

"Pretty good. I hung out with Cynda for
a bit," I replied, catching the grimace on your

face in the mirror's reflection before I stepped
into the shower stall. "She had me running her
around town since her car is in the shop."

"Why didn't you just let her borrow
your car?" you inquired as you slipped into
the shower behind me, wrapping your arms
around my waist.

Chuckling, I stated, "What I do with my
property is *my* business."

Feeling your hands slip away from me, I
turned around to face you. Taking your face
into my hands, I kissed you passionately as the
hot water cascaded over us. Your knees weak-
ened at the touch of our lips. Lowering myself
to my knees, my hands glided down your body
from your perky nipples to your throbbing clit.

"Oooo…" you moaned as my tongue tap
danced on your moist walls. "Oh Baby!"

Hiking your right leg over my left shoulder, you position yourself to allow my entry
into your pleasure zone. Ferociously, I sucked
your juices free from captivity to the sound of
your gasps and screams of passion. As the water
began to lose heat, I was just getting warmed
up. Rising to a standing position, I commanded,
"Go to bed."

Without question or hesitation, you

followed my orders, scampering out of the bathroom, grabbing a towel to dry yourself. Following behind you, I walk straight over to the queen size bed, stopping at the foot. You dabbed me dry with the towel, kissing me here and there.

Once I'm sufficiently free of all liquids outside my body, I needed to replenish my inner fluids. Before I could turn to step toward your kitchen, you turned me around to kiss you.

"Thank you, Baby. I needed that!" you giggled.

Smirking, I said, "Who doesn't need a little head to help them go to sleep? Need anything from the kitchen?"

"Just you," you winked before bouncing Tigger-style into the bed.

Shaking my head at your goofiness, I exited the bedroom to retrieve a beverage for myself. Standing naked in the middle of your kitchen, I could hear my cellphone ring in your bedroom. Never one to hide what I'm doing, I didn't rush back to answer the call. As I returned to your bedroom, I heard the last notes of my Love's ringtone from her third phone call. Sauntering over to my side of the bed, I anticipated your interrogation as I checked my messages. I double checked my phone to make sure my alarm was set before I slid under the sheets behind you.

"Was that Cynda?" you asked tentatively as I spooned you.

"Yes. I forgot to let her know that I arrived here safely. She said to tell you she's sorry if she interrupted us," I replied, relaying my text conversation. "I turned the ringer down so we shouldn't be disturbed again."

Tensing up in my arms, you asked, "Are you staying all night?"

"Are you kicking me out?" I replied nonchalantly.

"No!" you exclaimed as you turned your body to face me. "I want to wake up in your arms!"

"You know I have my meeting in the morning," I reminded you. "I'll be gone before you wake up."

"Can I persuade you to be late?" you asked as you kiss my lips, neck, nipples, and torso.

Laying on my back, I enjoyed your attention to the details of my body.

HIM

He was a simple man. Didn't ask for much in return as long as his lover was satisfied. He would move heaven and earth for her happiness. And she would do that times infinity for him. They were made for each other. An open minded soul, he wasn't surprised when she informed him of her pansexuality. After all, they met in a swingers chat room. He was, however, stunned when she explained why she would never marry him, or *anyone* for that matter.

"I love EVERYONE and I don't want to limit myself to one when so many can benefit from my Love," she said. "Unless you're saying yes to an open marriage that encourages me to date other men and women, that subject is closed."

Rather than stress himself wondering who she was loving night after night, he confessed that she would be his main lover but what's good for the goose is good for the gander and if his goose needed to wander, who was he to stop her when he can join her?

"I think I may have found a couple," she

said lustily in between wrapping her lips around his dick and fondling his balls. "He's definitely down but she's a little shaky. He asked me to give him a little time to talk to her about our offer."

Enjoying the pleasure he was receiving, he didn't want to fuck up the mood with questions but they were growing louder in his head, dampening his mood which she immediately took notice of.

Looking up at him sternly, she asked, "Is there something on your mind, Master? You seem... perturbed." Gently, she squeezed the evidence in question, his limp shaft in her hands.

"I thought it would be easier to find a couple to join us. This is taking too long," he admitted sorrowfully. He hated to show displeasure in her presence when it wasn't her doing. She couldn't help it that more men were open to group sex than the women they are involved with. "Maybe we should try a different approach. A single man and a single woman. The same rules will apply."

Smiling broadly at him before returning to her task of pleasuring him, she replied, "Yes, Master!"

Allowing himself to enjoy his blow job, he lay his head back onto the sofa. As his face contorted with images of extreme pleasure, he imagined his lover and himself with another couple.

They can start off making love to each other while my Lady and I watch for a while before doing the same in the adjoining bed. His girl wants what my Lady is receiving from me so she walks across the room to join us. Her man plays with himself, watching his girl give me head while I'm eating my Lady out. His girl gets jealous of my Lady's moans and pushes her aside so that she can sit on my face. Not to be left out, my Lady sits on her man's face. The riding competition ends with my Lady cumming all over her man's face through multiple orgasms. I stop eating to watch my Lady's reactions, grinning more with each rhythmic jerk of her slim body.

"UGGGGGH!!!" he moaned soulfully.

He looked down to see that he had cum all over his Lady's face. The smile on her face let him know that she had accomplished her mission.

Following his lover to their master bathroom, he inquired, "So what do you know about this couple?"

Turning the hot water on full blast, she stepped aside to allow him to enter the shower stall. Handing her lover a washcloth, she began, "They haven't been together very long but he's the one who approached me first. He was in the same chat room where I met you."

Soaping himself from head to toe, he listened intently as his lover explained that the man was desperately trying to bring some kind of spark to his relationship before he proposed to his girlfriend.

"He said he wants a full test drive before he puts himself down for the count," she laughed heartily before washing her face with Noxzema. "His words."

The discussion of marriage always left a bad vibe on his lover so he chose to refrain from adding his opinion on the other man's motives for swinging with them. If he felt assured that his comments would not initiate an argument, he would have pointed out that the man acted as if he was looking for a legitimate way to have multiple sex partners which usually led to infidelity based in selfishness. As he had been cheated on countless times before, he had no intention of enabling others in their infidelity. She would counter with the man's transparency in discussing the opportunity with his girlfriend and that she would cease all contact if the girl-friend refused to give consent or participate.

"Have you met him or at least seen what he looks like?" he asked, curious about his Lady's potential swing partner.

"Yes, and I must say he is rather tasty!" she exclaimed, more exuberantly than he antici-pated.

"So y'all have already…" he began as he shut the shower off, muscles tensing in his neck and arms.

With wide eyes, she apologized as she handed him a bath towel. "Oh, Master, I would never have sex with someone you aren't aware of! No! We've been video chatting but nothing in person."

Feeling relieved, he continued his interroga-tion. "What about her, his… girlfriend? Wife?"

"Girlfriend," she replied definitively. "She's a thick natural beauty. You'll love her, Master!"

"And they're both swingers or he's trying to make her into one?" he inquired as he wrapped the bath towel around his waist before exiting the bathroom.

"According to him, they haven't actively swung together but you know how I enjoy a challenge," she giggled as she joined him in the master bedroom. "We'll work up to inviting them to The Den."

"We wouldn't want either of them to be uncomfortable or else none of us will have any fun," he warned.

"Agreed. Maybe I should meet with her myself to gauge her interest in us," she suggested. "If she completely backs out, do we start our search over or move forward with him?"

Excitement zigzagged through his body at the thought of his Lady with *two* penises to play with!

"As long as you get what YOU want, we'll do as you please," he stated firmly as he climbed into their king size bed.

Chuckling, she agreed as she slipped into the sheets to lay next to him. "Thank you, Master."

HER

"Thank you Master! YES!" she screams, piercing the silence of the condominium.

It was his turn to start their day with a kiss and the moment his eyes popped open, his lips were on hers. Sleeping in the nude was one of their quickly agreed upon rules so he simply rolled over and went to work. In fact, perpetual nudity was one of the biggest rules neither of them wanted to break for fear of the consequences. The moment they entered their Love Den, clothes were immediately expected to be removed. This wasn't a place for parties and entertaining unless sex was involved.

As much as they teased and pleased each other, they always enjoyed adding an extra partner or two to see who could make the other jealous first. He usually gave in simply because he truly wanted her to "win". Once she emerged from the ashes of a devastatingly sexually unfulfilled marriage, she vowed to never commit herself to only one person when she discovered that she had the world to choose from. If she didn't fulfill all of his sexual desires, he would've left her in that hotel room the first night they had sex. Initially, he was turned off by her foul mouth but that same mouth had skills he could never get any other woman to do to him. However, to hear that she never wanted to get married again was a sore spot for him in their arrangement.

To appease his desire for a wife, she shared a lady friend of their mutual choosing from time to time. Vetting them was the part she hated most because all she wanted was someone down to fuck her. Sometimes Master joined in. Other times he watched. No matter what, she came. But Master was on a mission. He wanted a wife that accepted the fact that he needed her too because a LOT was required to keep him satisfied. A monogamous life would never do for either of them. She was the only one that could keep up with him and the bonus for his future wife were the breaks she would provide with her presence.

"Oh Master! Yes! Eat my pussy! EAT MY PUSSY!!"

Flipping over onto his back, he positioned her to sit on his face, the king size bed supporting their weight. Frantically, she clawed toward the bedroom walls but they are just out of reach, leaving her helpless to his oral assault on her own walls until he swallowed a mouthful of her juices.

"I hate this! It's too early to leave!" she said in exasperation. A layer of sweat covering her entire body, she pulled the sheet and comforter over her head to escape the morning chill. "Ugh, I hate this!"

"No, you don't because if you did, you would say yes," he said, propping up on an elbow as he looked down on her, stroking his fingers up and down the length of her body.

He thinks the predawn rays are what make her growl under the covers. Instead, it's the repeat discussion of why she won't marry him.

"No work, just play," he said, gently nudging her head through the comforter.

"We have that now!" she said, her voice amplified after pulling down the covers, exposing her breasts, immediately bringing her nipples to attention in the chilled room. "Except there's more to being a wife than fucking her husband and that's the only wifey qualification *I'm* offering! You can save that cooking/cleaning/birthing babies for someone else 'cause it won't be me!"

She had gone too far. She knew he didn't want to discuss marriage as long as her answer was not what he wanted to hear. Honestly, he opened the door, talking about "No work, just play" which was his reminder that his wife won't work if she doesn't want to. His biggest pet peeve was for his woman to be dissatisfied. As much as she hated to work for someone else, she felt more secure knowing that she was responsible for her own welfare. The last time she depended on a man, he spent more time working than being a husband to the point that he was too exhausted to give or receive sexual favors. If she was gonna do everything by herself, including pleasuring herself, there was no point in being married!

"We agreed not to crush each other's dreams," he said as he sat up to sit on the side of the bed. "I know you don't want to marry me. But I want to get married. I want to spend my life creating a home and a family with the woman I love who understands that I don't expect her to do everything by herself. You don't want to cook, clean or have any children. I respect that. I'm not asking you to do anything you can't or don't want to do.

Everything you do now is superb. As much as I want you to be happy, I have to be happy, too. I just need more than you're willing to give me."

"Do you really think you will find a woman that knows that you have a lifetime Mistress and will still marry you with the stipulation that I'm gonna fuck you, too?" she asked.

"Language, Mistress," he said, giving her a serious glare.

Shaking her head, she said, "The sooner you get a wife, the sooner you can stop trynna correct my *language*. You knew I had a filthy mouth when I first put my lips on your dick. Save your corrections for the Missus."

Sighing in exasperation, he said, "Agreed. And to answer your question, yes I do believe I will find a wife. I found *you*, didn't I?"

Her cell phone vibrated on the nightstand. As she reached for it, he prepared to shower before he left the house. A seductive grin spread across her face as she read the text message.

"We're in! When and where?!"

Quickly, she joined her lover under the water.

"I have excellent news, Master," she purred into his ear. "We found a couple."

Pulling her hand down toward his harden-
ing shaft, he kissed her passionately before she
dropped down to swallow his happiness.

ME

Clearing my calendar with Cynda was simple since she always knew whenever I spent time with you. I don't know where I will find the energy to put in a full day with you but for your birthday I will. It's the one day of the year that is all yours and the only gift you asked for was 24 hours with me. I know we can't fuck ALL day so I'll have to think outside the bedroom.

"Did you have any ideas of what you want to do for your birthday?" I asked as I kissed you good morning, my way. Gripping your thighs, I swirled my tongue in your pearl until Kitten purred "Good Morning Baby!"

"This is a good start," you said as you sat up in your bed. "Can we start with breakfast by the pool?"

"Anything in particular you want to eat?" I smirked, already anticipating your response.

"Hmm... I wanna keep it light. Just a couple of strips of turkey bacon and 2 slices of wheat toast," you smiled at me. "I can make the coffee."

"You'll do no such thing!" I said as I handed

you the TV remote control. "Sit back and relax. It's YOUR day!"

Although I didn't want to be tied down to one person, I knew how much you did and I couldn't let you spend your birthday alone. Some lucky someone is gonna be blessed to have you all to themselves. Until then, you pretend to be with me. I guess something is better than nothing, huh?

When I returned to your bedroom, I found you in the shower. Stripping down to nothing, I joined you. "Coffee is ready."

Turning to face me, you smiled seductively as you slid your body down until you were on your knees. Slowly, you drifted your hands down my chest and torso, meeting them together just inches below my navel. Looking down at you, I grinned as I watched your head slowly bobbing back and forth while your mouth worked it's magic on me.

"It's YOUR birthday and you're giving ME gifts?" I said, struggling to contain my balance in the shower stall.

With one last suckle, you rose to kiss me. "I wanted to thank you for spending my birthday with me. I really didn't want to be alone today."

Turning off the water, I wrapped you in a

body towel and gently kissed your cheek. "I got you, Baby. I know my signals are confusing. I don't want to be in a committed relationship with you yet I'm always there for you. I am human, ya know. I just don't want what *normal* humans want. Why commit myself to one person when there are so many out there to Love?!"

"OK, let's not worry about *us* and instead focus on ME!" "You said as you pulled me back into bed.

While you lounged by the pool sipping your first cup of coffee, I quickly prepared bacon and toast for us. My cell phone rang, prompting me to look at the nearest clock. 9:00 AM. Just like clockwork. Before you heard the second ring, I silenced the call by sending it to voicemail. "I told you I would be busy today. I reminded you before I left you breathless last night. I'll deal with you tomorrow."

Placing a tray over your lap, I am pleased to see the smile on your face. You sniffed the carnations as a tear rolled down your face. "You're so sweet!"

"What did I do?" I asked in confusion, sitting in a lounge chair beside you.

"You act like you can't be with me then you go and spend a whole day with me? Just because it's my birthday?" you asked.

Shaking my head, I said, "Babe, no one should be alone on their birthday. If you were with someone, I would fall back and get at you another day but I got you! You know that! Today, your wish is my command. Whatever you ask for, it's yours." Catching the glint in your eye, I added, "Except a commitment. Let's focus on happy thoughts today."

Slightly deflated, you replied, "You're right. I agree. Today is already going so well. Let's not spoil it." Before I could stop you, quickly you darted into the kitchen to put away the serving tray and your empty plate. When you returned to kiss me, you smiled. "Let's check out the latest exhibit at the art museum."

"Ah ha! A mutually beneficial experience. I knew I liked you for a reason. Good idea, Babe. Think about where you want to go for dinner and I'll make reservations."

While you go to your bedroom to get dressed, I take my cellphone into the kitchen to check my voicemail messages.

*"You have 1 message.

"When are YOU coming back? I need

YOU!"*

Rolling my eyes, I returned the call. "Meet me at the Den. Tomorrow morning. 9:00 AM." I knew if I said "We need to talk," I would find myself sitting alone for hours with avoided calls and texts. Experience is an excellent teacher and clearly a discussion must be had. "Give them what they want to get what I want" has always worked for me. No sense in derailing a good thing just because one player thinks they're out of the game. "They need to meet. Soon."

"I'm feenin' Jamaican food, Baby," you said as you entered the kitchen. I gawked at you as your stunningly statuesque body was hugged in a maroon and purple floral sundress, accentuating every sexy curve. Yoga does a body GOODLAWDHAVMERCY! "Can we go to…"

I cut you off with an adrenalized kiss. "I know just where to take you. For now, let's hit that museum or else we'll *never* leave this house!"

Biting your lower lip, you looked like you were contemplating your options.

YOU

You love me. You would do anything in the world for me if I would just give in to you. Little do I know, if I gave in, I would get everything I ever wanted from you in return. You can't wait to unleash the freak in you but you want to be in a committed relationship. One person to love and trust for the rest of your life.

But a threesome steps the game up a notch. You've been content with me but you know I need more. You've told me you don't want to lose me but I remind you that I'm not holding you captive. You're free to do whatever and whoever you want like I'm already doing. Since we've used protection since the day we first had sex, you know that I respect myself enough to protect all of my partners. You act like you're scared but how are you gonna be any kind of freak if you don't at least do what you want with the one person you DO trust with your body?

As you and I leave the art museum, you pulled me to you for a kiss. "I don't care if it's a man or a woman. I don't care if you know them or not. I want you and I want you to be happy. If it's ok with you, can we meet them for drinks first, to get to know each other better?" you asked.

"Just let me know when and where, Babe." I smirked.

"You already have someone in mind?!" you gasped.

Tilting your chin up, I replied. "You forget, I'm a swinger. I have a few possibilities for us. Like I said, let me know..."

Snatching yourself away from my embrace, you said stiffly, "I know. When and where."

"What's *that* face for?" I chuckled as I pulled you back into my arms before we continued walking to my car.

"Honestly, I'm uncomfortable. You *already* know someone to have a threesome with?!" you inquired, shakily.

"You sound like you want to ask me something. I have nothing to hide. Ask me anything!!" I encouraged with a squeeze to your waist.

We remained silent until we reached the passenger side of my car. Before I unlocked the door to let you in, you kissed me under my ear.

"Baby?" You looked up at me expectantly, hesitantly.

"Mmhmm…"

Our eyes locked on each other, your lips parted.

"N… no more questions. I trust your judgment," you exhaled. "Just one request."

"And that is?" I asked as I proceeded to unlock my car.

"Anyone but Cynda."

A blustery breeze cut between us as my hopes of one of my fantasies died from the reality that it was never coming true… with you…

Not wanting to go another minute further with doubts and secrets, I bluntly asked, "Why not Cynda?"

Looking at me incredulously, you snapped, "She's a liar!"

"One lie doesn't make her a liar. She's been truthful ever since, right?" I asked, softly kissing your lips.

"Yeah, but…" My kisses were throwing off your thought process. "But she lied to you too and I hate anyone that hurts anyone I love!"

"Did you forget that *you* have lied to me? Look. I'm OK. No harm done. She just didn't know how to handle the situation. She felt like she was cheating on me by talking to you but like I've told you, she's free to see whoever she wants as long as she's protected if they have sex," I explained. "As an ethically non-monogamous person, all I ask is that my partners are taking the same precautions with their other lovers that they would take if they were making love to me."

"For the record, I never had sex with her," you confessed.

"I know. Cynda told me everything," I grinned. "That's why I'm still with you. You told me the same thing she did. Plus, I haven't put rings on either of you so if you ever want to play with her, you have my permission, not that you need it."

Looking down at the ground, you said, "Maybe I need to talk to her. Although I'm not sexually attracted to her anymore, I did want to be her friend once."

"I'm sure she'll love hearing from you," I encouraged, hopeful that you would finally get along with my girlfriend. "Let me get you home so you can get ready for dinner. I'll come back in an hour to pick you up or do you need more prep time?"

"That's plenty of time, Baby. We can stop by your place first so you can pick up a few things to bring over and you can get ready with me," you hinted as I opened the passenger side door.

Smirking at your slickness, I sidestepped you. Starting the car engine, I stated, "Your place is closer to here and the restaurant. It makes no sense for me to go home to get stuff to take to your place. I don't want to leave anything behind and as soon as I walk through your door, you wanna have sex which will make us take longer to get ready. We won't be at the restaurant until ten!"

Laughing, you replied, "As long as the kitchen is open, they'll feed us!"

"Yeah, they'll feed us because we'll be there early enough to be fed. Did you want to eat dessert at the restaurant or do you want me to stop at Baskin-Robbins and get you a little something something?" I offered.

"Mmm, dessert?" you purred as your hand rubbed up my thigh. Not at all distracted, I kept my hands on the steering wheel and my eyes on the road as you proceeded to go down on me.

HIM

There she was.

After hours of not seeing her, left only with the *hope* of receiving her touch tonight, he found her. In his favorite restaurant. With someone else.

"Fuck. Me!" he thought to himself.

Debating whether to confront or observe, he chose to continue observing. Their exchange seemed mostly friendly. Nothing to be alarmed of if he were her only love which he clearly is not. Just when he's convinced that he witnessed nothing more than a couple of friends enjoying a meal, the waitstaff approached their table with brownie à la mode and their corporate mandated birthday song rendition.

"She's celebrating with a friend. She's human after all! Maybe she has a little bit of love in her heart that she can find a place for me…" he thought to himself.

Just as he's getting lost in his thoughts, a waitress approached him as he sat at the corner of the bar.

"Sir, that table asked if you would like to join them," said the waitress, pointing back at her table.

He looked over to see her smiling at him, waving him over. Happily surprised at the invitation, he accepted and joined the couple.

"Well, I know it's not *your* birthday," he says as he smiles at her before focusing on her companion. Extending his hand, he says, "Happy Birthday…"

"Tracy," replied her companion. "Thank you. Won't you join us?"

"Don't mind if I do," he says as he pulls a chair to the table, placing himself between the friends. "I don't mean to intrude on your celebration but I was just stopping in to get dinner as it looks like I will be alone tonight." He glanced at her as she briefly lowered her gaze from him.

"Oh, I'm sorry to hear that!" Tracy exclaimed. "Such a shame you don't have plans, a man as handsome as you."

When her eyes diverted in shock toward Tracy, he was intrigued. He was appreciative of the compliment and made sure she was aware of it.

"Thank you, Beautiful. My solitude will be

temporary but it still hurts to be alone. I'm the type of guy that likes to curl up with my lady in front of a roaring fire while we kiss and drink wine by candlelight. But that's just me." Every word he said drew Tracy in closer to him. He watched for her reaction to change but instead he found her smiling.

"Do you like her?" she asked.

He looked from her to Tracy. Taking in physical features alone, Tracy was essentially ideal for him. If she could possibly provide what his Mistress refused to deliver, indeed he liked her!

"Yes!" he exclaimed.

"Good," she smiled at him. Taking Tracy's hand into hers, she says, "I found our threesome partner."

HER

"Tracy, this is the friend I was telling you about, Xander," she smiled as he looked from her back to Tracy. "Xander, this is my friend, Tracy. She's interested in joining us at the Den."

His eyes lit up immediately. "I wasn't prepared to meet her tonight... I... I..."

Putting her hand on his arm, she said, "Your presence, although unexpected, was instead most fortunate in saving all of us the time of setting up an initial meeting. Of course, we can't go into much detail *here*. Suffice it to say, everyone is in accordance. We just need to decide when."

"Is tonight too soon?" asked Tracy with exuberance. She seemed surprised by the question until Tracy's explanation. "Today is my 30th birthday and I want a threesome."

Looking at her, Xander said, "I don't have any plans tonight so I'm available. As long as I can keep my 9:00 AM appointment tomorrow, I'm down."

"Tonight is fine for me as well. However, before we depart, I need you two to know something. Obviously, I am the mutual friend amongst us. I've known you both about the same length of time and based on what I know, you two will enjoy each other immensely. You both have similar desires which is why I have brought you two together.

"Tracy loves me dearly and wants me to settle down with her. So does Xander," she said, evoking a look of shock from both Tracy and Xander. "I am not the *wifey* type and I never will be. Instead, I have happily accepted my role of Lover and Mistress, respectfully. As much as you both love me, I am aware of how difficult it will be for either of you to find a mate that will accept that as long as you want me, I will be in your life. I'm not saying you will nor am I expecting you two to fall in love with each other and get married but until such time, you can both have fun with me."

Tracy and Xander looked at each other before looking at her.

"I thought we were looking for a couple!" they exclaimed in unison, much to their surprise.

Taking Xander's hand, she said, "On our first night, when you expressed your desire for marriage, I thought for sure that we wouldn't last long. But then I met Tracy. She's every-thing you want from me that I won't give you. And if she so desires, I will share her with you."

Taking Tracy's hand, she said, "As much as you love me and have done everything you can to keep me happy, I want to do the same for you. However, I can't give you EVERYTHING you need which is why I am introducing you to Xander.

"The only thing I offer to both of you is my body. Nothing more. Nothing less," she finishes.

Sitting in stunned silence, Tracy and Xan-der looked confusingly from her to each other and back.

"I don't know what to say..." said Tracy. "Yes, I love you and I knew you had other lovers but I never knew one of them could be a man!"

"And I was under the impression that we wanted a couple to join us, no offense to Ms. Tracy," stated Xander. "The more the merrier?"

"Master, if Tracy fits with us, we can always find someone else to join us. Besides, you were the one that suggested a single woman," she reminded him.

"I also suggested a single man although that is neither important nor a requirement. A single woman will be satisfactory," said Xander.

"Thanks?" replied Tracy in confusion.

"I don't mean to offend you, Tracy," said Xander as he took her hand. "We were looking for a couple to join us which has already proven to be difficult. And, to be honest, I would prefer a woman as opposed to a male partner but I am open to pretty much anything."

Blushing, Tracy said, "Well, I was expecting another woman but I'm not disappointed by the substitute."

"Then it's settled. Tracy, I'll take you back to your house to get your car so you can follow me to The Den," she announced.

"Can't I just ride with you?" Tracy asked nervously.

"Yes but if you want to leave before I do, I don't want to keep you waiting," she replied.

"I would prefer to go with you," Tracy said, clearly expressing her anxiety.

"OK Baby, you can ride with me," she purred, patting Tracy's hand.

"You two go on ahead and get ready. I'll take care of your bill," said Xander as he reached for his wallet.

Without a word, she sultrily walked out of the restaurant with Tracy trailing along behind her.

ME

Never one to doubt myself, I knew my plan would work. Tracy and Xander are perfect for each other. And they're both perfect for me. What I won't do for them, they can do for each other. Everyone wins!

Looking over at Tracy, I can see that she is pouting. "What's wrong, Baby?"

"That's who you're with when you're not with me?" Tracy asked with an annoyed tone.

"Sometimes," I admitted honestly. "You knew there were others. I never lied to you, Tracy."

"You never said you fucked men!" Tracy snapped, catching me off guard. If we didn't have someplace to be and someone waiting for us, I would've taken her home to fuck that anger out of her. Tracy was rarely pissed at me but I was usually in a position to physically relax her when bad vibes presented themselves. Since I was behind the wheel of my 2014 BMW 328i, I couldn't exactly do this *my* way. I was trapped into a conversation.

Fuck. Me.

"Why are you upset? We're not together in a committed relationship. Who I spend my time with is really none of your business unless I choose to share that information with you which I don't do because I know how you feel about me. And that was why I didn't say anything before now about anyone. Whether they were male or female shouldn't make a difference since you shouldn't be concerned with who I'm with when I'm not with you because I always use protection if anything goes down," I reminded Tracy.

"After tonight, you and I are done," Tracy stated quietly. Clearing her throat and speaking a bit louder, she continued. "I didn't realize how strong my feelings were for you until you told me Xander loves you too! I'm not going to be your mistress!"

Laughing, I said, "Exactly! I'M the Mistress! No one is cheating on anyone and everyone gets to play! Xander and I have a special arrangement. He and I are both highly sexual souls yet his appetite, oddly enough, is more insatiable than mine. That's why we need you. Between the two of us, we can make him happy."

"Do you love him?" Tracy asked quietly.

I took a moment to ponder the question.

"Love is a strong word and what I feel for Xander is what I feel for you. I love you both physically and I can't say 'I love you' like that but I can say that I love having sex with you."

I attempted to take Tracy's hand but she snatched it away. "I've NEVER had sex with you! I've always made love to you because *I love you!*"

Rolling my eyes as I turned off the highway, I drove quietly toward the gated community where the Den was located. Just outside the entrance, I parked my car and turned off the engine.

Tracy spoke silently. "I can keep up with you but if you need my help, what makes you think he'll be satisfied by the both of us?"

"First of all, I satisfy him sufficiently. He's the type of man that goes for what he wants and gets it. I have been his biggest challenge in that he can't get me to marry him. Otherwise, I make all of Xander's dreams come true!" I stated confidently. "You wanted us to take things up a notch. Your idea was making us an official couple. My idea is adding an extra partner every now and then, your choice."

"But I didn't choose *him*!" Tracy exclaimed.

"Excuse me but who's idea was it to have

a threesome on their 30th birthday with him tonight? That would be you. All I did was tell you about him. Once you laid eyes on him, you damn near came in your panties when he sat down at the table. So tell me again who chose him?"

"Um… um…" Tracy stammered. "Well you didn't exactly say no!"

"Why would I turn down the opportunity to have a ménage à trois with two of my favorite lovers when it falls so lovely into my lap?" I grinned as I slid my middle finger up and down Tracy's thighs, reaching further into her skirt with each stroke.

"Did you hear what I said? After tonight, you and I are done," Tracy repeated, trying to sound brave but I could hear the fear in her voice. Fear that I'll call her bluff. Fear that she won't have the strength to follow through.

Stopping my hand on Tracy's upper thigh, fingernail gripping the edge of her panties, I whispered, "I heard you but I don't believe you'll leave me. However, I do believe that if you do this with me, you will expect me to give everyone else up and commit only to you."

When I see Tracy's eyes light up, I am saddened to know I am right. The last thing

I wanted to do was give her false hope but I really wanted to fuck her. With or without Xander, I wanted Tracy. She was everything that I wanted in a woman. Loving. Caring. Kind. Considerate. Generous. Giving. Soft. Sexy. Shy. I know there's a freak in there. The more I gave to her, the more she gave to me. Would it be *that* bad to be with one person?

"We can talk about that after tonight. And if you don't want to do the threesome or if you want to do it with someone else, I'll understand. I'm not trying to ruin your birthday so we'll do whatever you want," I purred, thumping my finger against Tracy's clit, moistness increasing with each tap.

Smiling seductively, Tracy said, "Let's go to the Den. I want you to... Make. Love. To. Me. In front of Xander. Let him watch us. That's what I want for my birthday."

I did NOT see that one coming!

I swirled my finger a little further inside her pussy before I pulled it out and sucked on it. "If that's what you want, that's what you'll get."

Starting the engine, I thought of Xander's reaction to Tracy's change in his plans.

"I have an appointment in the morning at 9 AM," I said as I pulled into the garage next to

Xander's 2014 Jaguar XK convertible . "If you need to leave early, you can take my car. Xander can drop me off."

"I'm not leaving here without you," Tracy said as she took my hand before we walked into the condominium.

YOU

You followed me out of the garage into the spacious kitchen where we found Xander waiting for us. In his hands, he held a bouquet of flowers and a card. Assuming they were for me, you scowled at Xander until he spoke.

"Welcome to our Love Den," he said as he handed you the flowers followed by the card. "And again, Happy Birthday."

Taken aback at his courtesy, you replied "Thank You!" before opening the card. A wave of embarrassment covered you as you saw that Xander had given you a "Happy 1st Birthday" card. Smiling, you looked up at him, showing me the card. "Cute."

When Xander and I exchanged furtive looks at each other, you felt the need to "mark your territory" by pulling me to you for a kiss. Grabbing the back of my head, you gently pulled my hair back and whispered in my ear, "You are mine tonight."

Gripping your ass, I probed my tongue into your mouth to dance with yours. Xander took a seat at the table, observing our activity.

Slowly, I stripped you naked in the middle of the kitchen. Once I have you in your birthday suit, I lifted you up onto the kitchen island, parted your thighs and dove in. You leaned back on your elbows, attempting to get away from me. Allowing you to squirm a bit more, I sucked and licked just your clit until you scream my name. Satisfied with your response, I helped you down from the counter to lead you to the downstairs bathroom. After I turned on the shower, Xander poked his head into the door. "I'll go ahead and get the Den ready."

You rolled your eyes in annoyance at Xander's appearance but that emotion is short lived when I began undressing to join you under the water. Cupping your breasts in my hands, I kissed you softly on the nape of your neck and whispered "Happy Birthday, Baby." You softly moaned "I love you, Boo." Sliding my hands down to your torso, I stopped when my fingertips reached your clit. Again you moan. Fingering your pussy, we stood under the water as we washed away your fears and anxiety. After tonight, you are convinced that I will be all yours.

Turning off the water, you turned around to kiss me. "Make love to me. Now."

You rarely make demands and it IS your birthday so I took your hand and led you to the master bedroom of the three-bedroom condominium. As we walked down the hallway, we passed Xander sitting naked in the living room jerking off while watching girl on girl porn. You turned your nose up at the vision.

When we entered the bedroom, you gasped. Xander had set up the bedroom by lighting lavender scented candles all over the room and sprinkling red rose petals on the bed.

"Was this for you two?" you asked, sounding irritated.

"Baby, this was for all three of us. You wanted a threesome and I wanted to make it memorable. I know how you love romance and I thought this would be a nice idea," I explained. "I asked Xander to set this up."

Lowering your gaze, you said, "This was YOUR idea?"

"Yes. For you," I replied with a kiss.

"Oh Baby! I love you!" you smiled before you passionately kiss me.

"And since it's your birthday, you can run the whole show," I smirked.

A lascivious grin spread across your face. With one hand, you gently pushed me down onto the bed before you slowly climbed on top of me. Lovingly, you kissed my ankles, calves, knees, thighs, belly button, and nipples before once again you kissed my lips. As you hovered over me, you breathlessly exhaled, "Let's make love."

Taking your face into my hands, you gently lowered yourself on top of me as I pulled you in for a kiss. Once we were skin to skin, your first target are my nipples because you loved to see them stand at attention from your touch. As you swirled the tip of your tongue around each areola, I couldn't hold back my soft coos and moans. My hands softly stroked your head as your mouth worked it's way downward. Grabbing a handful of each breast, you gently squeezed them before sucking on each one. Knowing how ticklish I am, you carefully nibbled your way down my stomach to my clit. Cautiously, you nibbled along the edge of my walls before diving your tongue inside for a taste.

"Whoa!" I exhaled as you take me by surprise. Although you've pleasured me before, generally I'm the giver and you are the receiver. Considering it's YOUR birthday, I am a bit confused about the role reversal!

"Damn Baby!" I moaned aloud.

"Is this my pussy?" you asked me.

No... don't say it!

Munching more intensely, you gripped my thighs as I tried to get away from your oral assault. Again you ask, "Is this my pussy?"

"Mmm... Baby..." I growled.

I can't give in but dammit Baby you are working me out!!! As I tried to reposition us to 69, you added your fingers to the party! I don't know where you got the strength to do it but you kept me pinned to the bed, repeatedly asking "Is this my pussy?!"

Clearly, I have taught you well as you won't let up on me until you get the answer you desire. Enjoying the pleasure, fighting the urge to give in, I am torn. Physically my pussy IS yours anytime anyplace but I knew what you were asking and I'll be damned if you put me into a sex coma and make me say "I love you."

That's MY job!

Licking, sucking, clit flicking and tongue filled kisses continue for over an hour until finally I can't take anymore. As I writhed in ecstasy, you informed me, "This pussy is all mine, Baby! I don't want him to touch it. I don't want him to smell it. I don't even want him to

SEE it cuz it's all MINE!" You eat me until I damn near cry because it feels so damn good!

"It's yours Baby! It's yours!" I exclaimed loudly.

Crawling up the bed to curl up next to me, you kissed me softly on the lips, allowing me to taste myself on your tongue. As I drifted off to sleep, I heard you whisper, "I'm gonna make you love me!" I smiled to myself as I mentally wished you good luck.

HIM

He always knew she had other lovers. He didn't care as long as she came back to him. He just assumed their new lover would be new for *both* of them. And he never imagined her friend would be so open to a threesome so quickly!

Then again, my Mistress fucked me the night we met only for us to later discover that we had already met online in a swingers chat room!

"My God how did I get blessed to find TWO of them! As much as I love Mistress, I never thought I could find a partner for us and she already loves my Mistress! Even if Tracy doesn't want me, as long as she's around, my Mistress will be happy!" he thought to himself.

"They're here!" he said with excitement as he heard the alarm system indicating that someone was in the garage. He entered the kitchen with a bouquet of daisies and a birthday card, gifts to welcome their guest. Just moments later, Mistress is followed in by Tracy.

He took in Mistress' full beauty as her attire was blocked by the table at the restaurant and he was too busy checking out Tracy's ass on her way out of the door. As Mistress caught his gaze, she winked back at him. Just as he was about to ask the ladies if they were ready to begin, Tracy kissed Mistress. Grabbing the back of her head, Tracy pulled Mistress's hair back and whispered in or nibbled on her ear. When Mistress gripped Tracy's ass and passionately kissed her, his dick immediately hardened as he took a seat at the table and observed their activity, grabbing on himself as Mistress stripped Tracy naked in the middle of the kitchen. When Mistress lifted Tracy up onto the kitchen island, parted her thighs, and started eating her out, he leaned in for a better view. He grinned when Tracy screamed out Mistress's real name. When the ladies finished part one of the evening, he patiently waited and followed them to the bathroom. After he heard that the shower had been turned on, he poked his head into the door. "I'll go ahead and get the Den ready," he announced.

Lighting scented candles to set the mood in the bedroom, he smiled as he sprinkled blood red rose petals onto the bed. When he heard the shower turn off, alerting him to know that the ladies will be in the room soon, he stepped out to go to the living room. To occupy his time while Mistress had her way with Tracy, he sat naked in the living room jerking off while watching girl on girl porn to get himself ready to join the action. All he needed was the signal from Mistress then HIS fun with the ladies would begin.

Over an hour passed when he became bored after watching three flicks. Suddenly he heard Mistress exclaim, "It's yours Baby! It's yours!"

"They should be ready for me by now," he thought to himself. When he approached the bedroom door, he didn't hear a sound. No moaning. No panting. Nothing. Quietly turning the doorknob, he peeked inside to see Mistress curled up in Tracy's arms.

"Hmm… To join them or not to join them, that is the question," he thought to himself as he entered the room.

In her sleep, Tracy shifted slightly to pull Mistress closer to her before kissing her on the top of her head. He felt a slight twinge of jealousy but quickly dismissed the emotion. Opting to sleep in another room, he reluctantly allowed the ladies their rest.

"They're gonna need it," he smirked to himself.

HER

Her eyes peeked open when she felt an extra presence in the room. He was standing at the foot of the bed, watching her and Tracy. He hesitated a moment before leaving, as if he wanted to wake them. Instead, he quietly walked out of the bedroom. Shortly afterward, she heard the TV being turned on to ESPN.

Sighing, she looked over at the clock on the dresser. 2:34 AM. She knows he is disappointed that he didn't get to join in their fun but it's Tracy's birthday, the one day of the year she fully dedicated to her lover. Scooting her butt closer to Tracy, she drifted back to sleep.

The next morning, she rose from the bed, stretching her naked body to it's fullest extension. Looking back at the bed, she smiled as she observed Tracy sleeping peacefully. As she walked out of the bedroom, her senses detected that Xander was also awake. With a demure smile on her face, she joined him on the couch with memories of the previous night dancing in her head.

"Did our guest enjoy her evening, Mistress?"

he asked without looking at her.

"Yes she did," she replied, anticipating the next question.

"Do I still have an appointment at 9?" he inquired.

Smiling broadly, she glanced at her watch. Just as the digital readout changed from 8:59 AM to 9:00 AM, she climbed on top of him and said, "Yes, you do."

His hands grasped her ass as she easily slid down onto his rock hard dick. As he was her only male partner and after regular testing due to her activity with her girlfriends, he was the only partner that she had unprotected sex with. A moan of satisfaction escaped his lips as she worked her hips to get all of him inside her. Their rhythmic movements made the sofa creak quietly as SportsCenter played in the background. She gripped her thighs closer to his body as she fought the approach of first of many multiple orgasms. She knew she would come again soon but she wanted him to come first.

"Oh Mistress!" he growled as he held her closer to his body. "Damn your pussy is so wet!"

"Kitty was excited to see you, Master," she purred in his ear.

"Not as excited as I am to see her..." he replied with a kiss before he lay down on the sofa. "...and you!"

Slowly, he ground his hips into hers, making her moan softly. Deeper and deeper he went, further than ever before!

"Has he been holding back on me all this time or is he on Super Viagra?! He's bigger and harder than ever!" she thought to herself. Suddenly, her body began seizing as she allowed the first round of orgasms loose. Just as she reached the peak of her climax, he came inside her.

Spent and exhausted, they lay in each other's arms and cuddled.

"If I continue to consent to your unrestricted freedom to be with other lovers, will you marry me?" he asked.

Grimacing, she inquired, "Are you saying you want an open marriage?"

"Yes," he said as he smiled at her.

She was visibly shaken. She never believed he would change his mind. As much of a control freak as he can be, could he really be truly happy knowing he couldn't control who she slept with?

"What do you say?" he asked expectantly.

Looking into his eyes, she said, "Let me

think about it."

"OK…" he replied hesitantly. "If it'll help you make your decision, I'm in love with you and all I want is for you to be happy. You can keep Tracy or anyone else you want. I just want you."

She stared into his eyes looking for any sign of deception but all she saw was his love for her. She hadn't seen a look like that since her first marriage. Suddenly, she felt agitated.

"Like I said, I'll think about it," she stated as she gently pushed on his chest. "I need to wash up before I take Tracy home."

Reluctantly, he allowed her to retreat to the hallway bathroom.

Confused by her emotions, she looked at her reflection in the bathroom mirror.

"He said yes to everything I want, including Cynda and Tracy. Except he wants kids…" Placing her hands on her belly, she said, "…but I can't give him any."

Slumping down to the floor, she silently sobbed.

She never imagined he would give in to her demands in exchange for marriage. She thought for sure the idea of his wife sleeping around would be a major turnoff. Now she felt trapped because she never told him she couldn't conceive children. Once her physician confirmed her barrenness, she felt that much more free to have multiple sexual liaisons as she was no longer afraid of an unintended pregnancy.

"I'm going to lose Xander," she said quietly to herself as she rocked herself on the floor, the cold tile under her ample cheeks keeping her cool and calm.

YOU

You wake up to me kissing you softly on the cheek.

"Time to get up Sleeping Beauty. Did you want me to make you some brunch before I take you home?" I asked.

Sitting up groggily, you squinted your eyes at me. "What time is it?"

"Nearly noon," I replied without glancing at my watch.

Fully alert, you looked up at me. "Is he here?"

Shaking my head, I said, "No, he went for a jog. Should be back in less than an hour."

"Oh…" You smiled at me seductively. "So we have the whole house to ourselves?"

Seeing where your thoughts were headed, I grinned back, "For the moment."

Patting the space beside you, you said seriously, "Good because you and I need to talk."

"Ruh roh," I said with a giggle as I chose to sit at the foot of the bed. The look on your face immediately told me this would be a serious conversation and I didn't want to be within slapping distance. "What's up, Baby?"

"So did you tell him I'm the one you want?" you asked, drumming your fingers on your chin.

Looking confused, sarcastically I said, "I wasn't aware that I had to choose between you two."

Angrily, you yanked the covers off of you, exposing your beautiful chocolate body. Kitty started purring at the distraction as you rose from the bed to stand in front of me. "You said last night that your pussy is mine!"

Sighing in exasperation, I wrapped my stems around your waist. "Baby, you know it's yours but it's his and Cynda's, too."

Glaring down at me, you said, "So you lied to me?"

"Lied?! When did I lie to you, Tracy?!" releasing you as I exclaimed in my defense.

"When you told me your pussy is mine," you said as you crossed your arms over your chest, bed sheets falling to the floor.

Sitting at the foot of the bed, I held my head in my hands. Looking up at you, I said, "Baby, you know it's yours."

"I told you last night that your pussy is all mine! Did you think I was playing when I said I don't want him to touch, smell or SEE it because it's all MINE?!" you screamed.

Looking up at you, I sternly said, "Go shower and get dressed. I'm taking you home."

"We're not done talking!" you snapped as I calmly rose from the bed.

"You're not talking at all. You're yelling at me and making demands of me that you know I won't honor," I said as I walked toward the door. "Hurry up. I want you out of here before he gets back."

"I don't give a fuck about him! I love YOU!" you exclaimed.

"You love *me* or the idea of who you want me to be?!" I asked incredulously. "Tracy, all you've done is try to manipulate me! You thought a threesome would make me choose you over him then you don't even go through with it!! You're too possessive for my taste and I don't want or need anyone trynna put me on lockdown. Especially a jealous insecure prude that has to be told every little thing to do! If I wanted that, I should've stayed with my ex-husband!"

Too far. I always go too far.

SMACK!!!

Quietly, you gathered your belongings before heading into the bathroom. With one last glance at me, you said, "I guess I was right... We're done..."

I rubbed my cheek as you left the room.

ME

Standing by the front door, I waited to take you home as I prepared to accept your resignation from our situationship. Watching you walk down the hallway, I mentally took screenshots of you in my mind. Your beautiful stride. The innocence in your smile. The light in your eyes. No point in reminiscing. You're done with me.

Holding your head down as you stood in front of me, you apologized. "Baby, I'm sorry. That's not how I want our hands to touch each other. Ever."

"You ready to go?" I asked coldly.

No doubt shocked by my harsh tone, you looked up at me. "Baby, I'm sorry for hitting you!"

Turning off the alarm before opening the door, I said, "Apology accepted. Let's go."

Reluctantly, you walked out of the door before I reset the house alarm to follow behind you. The drive back to your place was dead silent. Occasionally, I looked over at you to see you looking out of the window. To your surprise, I parked in your driveway without leaving the engine running. When I walked into your house, you broke the silence.

"Baby, I'm sorry that my insecurity is making me cling to you but I don't want to lose you! I love you!" you said as you looked at me expectantly.

Looking deep into your eyes, I said, "I always make sure we never do anything you don't want to do yet you're always trying to cross *my* boundaries. You say you want a relationship yet you're selfish and possessive. You have to have reciprocation and trust with your partner. You're willing to take. What are you gonna give or give up to be with me?"

"Why can't you just be with me and only me? Don't I give you everything you need?" you asked clutching my hands in yours.

"No, you don't," I replied. "Even though you've only seen me with Cynda, you've always known that I'm bisexual so what makes you think I won't still want the touch and feel of a man? That's why I have Xander. I'm not a lesbian, Tracy."

Visibly shaken, you asked, "Is he the only other person you want?"

Thinking of a potential swing partner, I admitted honestly, "No, there's a *couple* other people."

You walked over to the sofa to sit down. When you looked up at me expectantly, I sat beside you with space between us.

"Where do we stand now?" you inquired, turning to face me.

"According to you, we're done. Remember?" I reminded you.

"Baby, I never meant that! I don't want to lose you!" you exclaimed as you slid next to me.

"Tracy, you never had me. You had my pussy. You never had my heart," I admitted.

Looking dejected, you took my hands into yours. "I thought you loved me. I thought you wanted to be with me. I'm in love with you."

Caressing your cheek, I said gently, "You know how I feel about you. It's the same way I felt yesterday and the day before. But I'm not in love with anyone."

Looking slightly relieved, you quietly asked, "Have you *ever* been in love?"

Sitting back on the sofa, I pondered your question. "No, I guess I haven't been. I mean I loved my ex-husband but I can't say I was *in love* or else I would've fought harder for the marriage."

"Do you *want* to fall in love?" you inquired.

Chuckling, I said, "I've managed to survive this long without being in love so probably not."

Again, your smile faded.

I already had to have an exit interview with Xander. After my confession, I'm sure he'll be happy to let me go. As for you...

"Why am I here?" you asked, your voice shaking.

Leaning with my elbows on my knees, I looked over at you. "What do you mean?"

"Do you want *me*?" A tear rolled down your cheek.

Sighing, I knew where this was going. "Yes, I want you. For the same reason the first time you asked me. I love having sex with you."

"But you don't love ME?" Your eyes looked at me pleadingly.

"Not the way you want me to," I said with a slight frown. "Look, Baby. Let's not do this right now."

"No let's finish this now. I need to know before you walk out that door if you're my girlfriend or not!" you exclaimed.

Standing slowly, I looked back at you. "You couldn't handle being my girlfriend." Before I took one step, you took my hand.

"Whatever you want your girlfriend to do, I'll do it," you agreed.

Had I finally broken you? Were you finally ready to submit to me?!

"I keep Xander, Cynda, and anyone else I so choose," I offered. "Don't forget that I'm a swinger."

I knew it was hard enough on you when I left you alone. You just found out about two of my other lovers not to mention my side hobby. No sense in letting all of my skeletons out of the closet. Hell, I was willing to drop all of my side tricks if I could keep my Top Three. Cynda was down from day one. Except for the marriage thing, Xander was a lock. I just had to convince you how good this life could be!

"Which one of us will you live with?" you inquired, perking up.

"No need to change the current set up," I said, not wanting to set myself up to piss off any of my Loves. I preferred to keep what I needed at each location. The last thing I wanted was any one of them to keep track of me and my whereabouts. They saw me when they saw me and they were fine with that. That is until…

"Move in with me. You need a safe place to lay your head every night and I'm sure you could use a break from Xander, Cynda and me. I'll leave you your space. You can come and go as you please. It will just make me feel better knowing you're safe wherever you are," you suggested.

Content with your concern, I caressed your cheek. "Before I respond to that, what about Xander and Cynda?"

"And the swinging? Compromise: you can keep living your free spirit life if you move in with me," you proposed.

Smirking, I looked at you. "One, moving in with anyone negates the very idea of me being a *free* spirit. Two, be specific what you ask for, Tracy. You only get me here and there. You might not like living with me."

Standing up to kiss me, taking my hands into yours, you said, "I love you. Quit trying to change my mind."

Looking into your eyes, I said directly, "There's more to being my girlfriend than living with me"

"Don't forget loving you!" you grinned.

Chuckling, I replied, "And loving me. For one, the ultimatums and tantrums have to stop. We're both adults. Let's act like it."

"Yes, Mama," you smirked.

"Mama?" I asked with a raised eyebrow.

You nodded your head with a demure smile.

"You've never called me that* before. Hmm... I like it," I admitted.

"Is there anything else you like? Is there anything I can get for you or do for you?" you offered, gently squeezing my hands.

"Tell me what you expect me to do, as your girlfriend," I requested.

"Love me as I love you. Support me as I support you. Have fun with me. Grow with me. Teach me how you want to be loved," you explained as you sat back down on the couch, urging me to join you. "Be faithful to me."

Raising my eyebrow, I looked at you.

"By that, I mean be 100% honest with me," you explained. "If you're no longer seeing Xander or Cynda or if you want someone new, please tell me. I already tell you my every move because I don't want you to worry about me. I just don't want to lose you, Baby."

"Understood. I can do that," I agreed.

Smiling, you looked up at me. "Does that mean I'm your girlfriend?"

Letting out a heavy sigh, I said, "Yes, you're my girlfriend."

Immediately, you threw your arms around

my neck, kissing me all over my face. "I got the best birthday present ever! You're my first girlfriend!"

For a brief moment, a wave of nervousness succumbs me. I knew I was your first same sex encounter but to be your first same sex partner was a deeper relationship.

Am I ready for this?! Better yet, are *you?*

"Before you sign on the dotted line, you are aware that this is an open relationship. I'm not stopping you from seeing someone else. I only ask that you protect us by protecting yourself," I said to let you know that I'm not halting you from having fun without me.

"I have the one I want. No need to look any further, Baby," you replied with a kiss. "I love you."

Feeling my lips were about to repeat your words, I quickly corrected myself and said "Mm hmm."

HIM

"Would you like to join me for dinner tonight?" he said, reading the text message aloud.

"She's going to say yes!" he thought to himself with a grin.

Her usual pattern for responding to his requests was easy to follow. If she wants to meet outside the Den, that meant she had agreed and they would go out to celebrate. If she wanted to meet at the Den, after she turned him down, she turned him on and out all through the night.

"We're getting married! We're getting married!" he sang to himself as he replied to her text message.

XAN69: Yes. Our usual place? Usual time?

Not necessarily wanting to turn down the option, he hesitated to ask about Tracy.

XAN69: Will Tracy be joining us tonight?

MSTRESS: Yes, our usual place and time. No Tracy. Just us for dinner. See you tonight at 7

Checking the time on his cell phone, he

calculated how much time he would need to prepare for his grand gesture. After a year of asking, he was finally going to get his Mistress to marry him!

Going through his walk-in closet to retrieve his dark blue Armani suit, he said to himself, "Now I know she's gonna try to weasel out of this, talking about she can't give me any children. Won't she be happy to hear that I don't want any!"

On the way to the restaurant, he stopped by the jeweler to pick up her engagement ring. He was so giddy with anticipation that he didn't need his car! He could've floated to see her! Mistress was like no other woman he had ever encountered. Her daredevil attitude in the bedroom introduced him to new pleasures he had never imagined he would ever experience in his life until he met her. In addition to her competitive sexual side, Mistress also had a giving heart as owner of "Aunt Missy's Healing House", a rooming house for victims of domestic violence. His devilish angel would soon become his wife!

He arrived at the restaurant just moments before she walked inside. Barely able to contain his excitement, he counted to ten before leaving his car to join her in the waiting area.

His face lit up at the sight of her. With a single blood red rose, he approached her.

"Good evening, Mistress," he said with a kiss to her hand before giving her the rose.

"Good evening, Master," she smiled back before sniffing the petals.

After the hostess announced that their table was ready, they quietly followed behind her. He was sure that his lover was checking out the hostess's ass but he was mesmerized by his Mistress.

Once they were alone at their table, he simply looked at her. She had her hair pulled up into a bun, showing off the slenderness of her neck. She was wearing the diamond tear drop necklace he bought her for her birthday that year.

Smiling, he began, "When you're being realistic, children don't exactly fit into our lifestyle. In fact, my family was the one that wanted me to have kids. I wanted them to be happy. Mom already said she's got plenty of grandkids so she'll be fine if I don't give her any. She just wants me to be happy. And I am, with you."

Looking stunned, she stared at him.

"I figured me wanting kids was the only

hold up to you saying yes," he smirked. "I'm letting you know that, unless you want them, I don't."

"I... I... don't know what... to say," she replied. "I mean... Kids are one thing but... what about Tracy? And Cynda?"

"You can have anyone you want to keep you happy," he said as he reached for her hand. "I only want you."

Her stunned expression was his cue. Not wanting to embarrass himself, he gently squeezed her hand to "ask".

"You don't want children and I can keep my girlfriends," she stated.

"The only thing that would change is that you would be legally bound to me, the only type of bondage you said you'll ever use again," he winked.

Slipping her hands out of his, she asked, "Why do we have to get married, Xander?"

"We don't HAVE to. I want to protect you and support you," he explained. "You don't have to be my wife for that but it would make your life easier. As much as you complain that you hated working for someone else and love being your own boss, I would think you would jump at the opportunity to live a more comfortable life. No cooking. No cleaning. No birthing babies. Just fun and pleasure for the rest of your life. With me."

Holding her head down, she said, "I know you really want this but I don't see the point in you marrying me. I'm not a monogamous woman."

"And I'm ok with that. I've known that the whole time we've been together so it's not breaking news," he said, struggling to keep smiling.

She let out a heavy sigh before looking up at him. "I like things as they are. If I marry you, you'll expect me to live with you. Tracy already has a fit when I see you so…"

"She can move in with us!" he offered. "Look, Mistress. I've removed all of your roadblocks. The only thing stopping us is *you*."

He could see the hesitation in her eyes. With one last effort he asked, "Why did you marry your first husband?"

Lowering her head, she said, "I just wanted him for sex. Until you, he was my best male lover. He was my first lover ever and I thought he would be the only one I needed. Then the sex got boring when I accepted the fact that I needed more than he was willing to give. I've never wanted to be unfaithful to anyone so I suggested a threesome. From that day forward, we were just counting the days until the divorce was final."

"Isn't that all you want from me? A sexy man with an insatiable sexual appetite focused solely on you?" he asked, gently squeezing her hands. "And I know I'm not enough for you. Keep Tracy, Cynda, or whoever you need to keep you happy. If you need to talk it over with them, I understand. Do whatever you gotta do. I'm offering you a fully polyamorous life with me. All I'm asking is for you to just say yes."

When she squeezed his hands in return, he was filled with hope.

"Let me consider your proposal, no pun intended," she said as a waiter approached the table.

HER

She was stunned. Xander and Tracy were both offering her everything she ever wanted: unrestricted fun with either of them and whoever else she wanted. Now that she had the full freedom to have anyone, she truly only wanted her Top Three.

He allowed her time to think things over while she was away on her week-long all-inclusive island vacation to Jamaica with Tracy, a belated birthday trip. Not wanting to ruin their holiday, she waited until their last night on the island before she told Tracy about Xander's marriage proposal.

"You have got to be the most desired woman on the planet! No sooner than I get lucky enough to have you as my girlfriend, Xander raises the ante with a marriage proposal!" exclaimed Tracy as she sipped on her Mai Tai with extra cherries. She gulped down the last of her rum and coke while she looked out at the sunset over the Caribbean Sea. "And you 'get to keep' me!"

"Glad you're so happy about this," she said

sarcastically. "Honestly, I thought you would be upset considering we just recently officially became a couple."

"You didn't break up with me to tell him yes. Hell! As long as I have you, you can marry the man in the moon for all I care!" Tracy said with a kiss.

"I really like Xander and the fun we have together but the last thing I'll do is let YOU go!" she declared, surprising herself.

Tracy looked over at her. She was still staring at the turquoise water. "Really?"

Her smirk turned into a full smile as she turned to face Tracy and took her hands. Simply, she said, "I love you, Tracy."

Looking shocked, Tracy stuttered, "Y-y-you l-l-love me?"

Chuckling, she said, "As much as I've tried to fight it, day by day I've been falling in love with you. The more you showed how much you wanted me and accepted me as I am, the deeper my feelings grew for you. You have accepted that I have to live a polyamorous life and you want to join me in it. How could I *not* love you?"

As tears rolled down Tracy's cheeks, she gently wiped each one away. Tracy pulled her in for a kiss. "I love you, too, Boo."

A couple of vacationers walked by as she and Tracy happily showed their love for all the world to see.

Reluctantly allowing Tracy to pull away from their embrace, she smiled as the thought of Xander crossed her mind.

"Baby, remember when I told you that love is a strong word and what I feel for Xander is what I feel for you?" she began.

Hesitantly, Tracy replied, "Yes…"

Gently squeezing Tracy's hands, she confessed, "I'm in love with him, too."

She expected Tracy to go ballistic but instead…

"I know," Tracy smiled. "As much as you try to keep him happy, I knew it was more than sex for you with him. and if you decide you want to marry him, I'm here as long as you want me. Somehow you've managed to keep him, Cynda, and me happy but what about you? What will make YOU happy, Mistress?"

She stood and pulled Tracy into her arms. "Having you, Cynda, and Xander in my life will keep me happy. And he wants me to be happy with you, her, and him."

"I'm not sure about moving in with y'all but

you have my blessing to marry him, if you felt you needed it," Tracy said with a kiss. "And I've talked to Cynda. We're cool again."

"Thank you, Baby. I wouldn't marry him without it," she said before passionately kissing her girlfriend and walking hand in hand back to their room to pack.

Before she left for her trip, she asked him to give her a couple of days after her return to give her time to think but he was the first person she wanted to see when she and Tracy returned. After taking Tracy home, she went to her place to drop off her luggage and freshen herself prior to driving to the Den. She wanted to surprise him with her early return and her response.

Entering the condominium, she was met by the sight of Xander dancing in the middle of the kitchen singing Justin Timberlake's "Mirrors". Smiling to herself, she waited a moment before clapping her hands at his performance. Grinning as wide as the great outdoors and without missing a step, Xander took her hand to twirl her around.

"My beautiful Mistress has returned!" he said before kissing her. "I thought you needed a couple of extra days away."

Fully allowing her love for him to flow, she replied, "I wanted to come home and give you my answer. Yes, Xander. I will marry you."

A look of relief covered Xander's face. "In that case, this belongs to you." Taking her left hand, he slipped a 5-carat solitaire Princess-cut platinum diamond ring onto her finger before pulling her to him for a kiss.

"There's something else," she says as their lips part. Looking up at him and smiling, she said, "I love you, Xander."

He smiled down at her. Without questioning her, he replied, "I love you, Mistress."

YOU

As reality sat in, you smiled at pictures we took of us on the beach in Jamaica.

"My girlfriend is getting married," you said to yourself.

Instantly, your smile faded.

*What kind of relationship can *we have if she's marrying Xander?*

"I'm Mistress's mistress," you smirked as you sauntered into your bedroom to put away your luggage. "Probably told him your answer and instantly started celebrating!"

A twinge of jealousy touched you as you imagined Xander between my legs. Licking my clit. Sucking on my walls.

Immediately, you grabbed your car keys and drove toward the Love Den.

"You are MINE, Mistress! Married or not, you are MINE!" you declared to yourself as you sped through the St. Louis city streets.

Arriving 20 minutes later, you pulled into the driveway behind Xander's car as it sat beside mine. Stifling a growl at the sight of his vehicle, you marched up to the front door. Praying that you won't upset me with your interruption, you held your breath as you waited for someone to answer the door.

"Tracy?!" Xander asked in surprise when he opened the door. Since he is fully dressed, you are relieved to know he hasn't been inside me recently. "What brings you here?"

"Is Mistress here?" you asked tentatively, listening out for my voice.

"Yes, she's just getting out of the shower," Xander said as he stepped aside to let you into the condo. "Is everything OK?"

Honestly, you replied shakily, "No."

Sitting quietly on the sofa, you gathered your thoughts as you and Xander waited for me to enter the living room.

"Baby? Are you OK?" I asked with concern as Xander and I sat on either side of you.

"No, Mistress! Everything is NOT OK! I don't know what I was thinking when I said you can have Xander. How can you be with the both of us?!" you exclaimed.

Taking your hand in mine, I said, "We will guide you. I know you were raised in a monogamous world but you deserve a polyamorous life. Yes, I'm marrying Xander but I'm still your girlfriend. Xander and I will give you all of the love, support and freedom you need to be happy."

"What can Xander do when all I want is *you*?!" you snapped.

"I can give you two time alone without my interference and I can help out when you need me. You're my metamour, Tracy. You are just as much my responsibility as Mistress," Xander explained.

"Metamour? What's *that*?" you asked as I wiped your tears away.

"A metamour is the partner of one's partner, with whom one does not share a direct sexual or loving relationship," Xander quoted from the polyamory website we use for additional information. "Since we don't have a sexual relationship with each other but we each have one with Mistress, that makes us metamours."

"I guess I'm still trying to wrap my brain around the fact that you can be with the all of us," you said as you lay your head on my shoulder. "I mean I guess we aren't cheating since Xander knows about us but…"

Smiling at you, I said, "I wish there was a simple way to explain this but I've always been poly so I can't fully grasp your anxiety about this."

"Maybe I can help," Xander said as he took your hand. "Before I met Mistress, I was 100% monogamous with any lady I was involved with although generally they weren't faithful to me. I never had a problem with them having other lovers. I hated that they lied to me about it. When I met Mistress and she explained polyamory to me, I was intrigued. All that time I had been cheated on and I could've lived happily ever while allowing my Lady her freedom to do as she pleased as long as she was transparent with me. Now I have the one woman that deserves that treatment."

"And he's free to date anyone he chooses as long as he's honest about their relationship and we all remain cordial," I explained.

Acknowledging the growing physical attraction you have toward Xander, you said, "So, if he wanted to, Xander can fuck me too?"

Smiling at you, I replied, "If he wants to, yes, he can."

Turning to face Xander, you stated, "I'm not saying I *want* to fuck you. I'm just trying to understand all of this."

"Understood," Xander grinned back at you. "Currently it's just us three in a vee dynamic with Mistress as the pivot. If you and I begin dating, we three will be a triad."

"Metamour? Vee? Pivot? Triad?! So many terms!" you gasped, overwhelmed.

"Oh, Baby, there's so much more to learn and we'll be there every step of the way," I said assuringly before I kissed you gently on the lips.

"I'm gonna give you two some time to talk," Xander said before kissing me and exiting the room.

"And it's perfectly fine with me if you like Xander," I admitted. "He's already expressed his interest in you."

"Interest? In what way?" you asked as you looked at me.

"He's still waiting for that threesome," I smirked with a wink.

"Oh…" you replied.

"He can tell you himself but he would like to see if there's more than a physical attraction," I explained as I stroked my hand up and down your thigh.

"I don't date men, Mistress. I just want to fuck them from time to time," you stated definitively. "If he's OK with being my Maintenance Man, cool. Otherwise, he's just your fiancé as far as I'm concerned. I don't want a man. I don't want another woman. I just want you."

"Did we answer all of your questions?" I asked gently.

"Yes. And I'm sorry," you said apologetically.

"Sorry for what, Baby?" I asked as I pulled you into my arms.

"For coming over unannounced and interrupting your celebration with Xander. I know he was ecstatic when you told him you said yes," you smiled.

"He's still on Cloud Infinity," I chuckled. "And I'm proud of him for being a supportive metamour to you. He's just as concerned for you as I am simply because I love you. And he and I will feel that way toward anyone else you date."

"Mistress..." you said as you rose from the sofa. "I don't want anyone else."

Giggling, I replied, "You say that now because you're all up under me. Wait until we go out and those ladies see that sexy gorgeous body and dazzling smile. You'll have a second girlfriend in no time."

"Thanks for the vote of confidence but unless she approaches me like you did, I'll be fine," you smiled as you sat on my lap. "By the way, did I ever thank you for that drink?"

Seductively, you ran your hand under my towel, slowly circling my nipples.

"Tracy..." I said as I started to relax. "Don't start what you can't finish."

"Boo, you know I'll finish," you purred as you led me to the bedroom where Xander was watching TV. Entering the room, to Xander's and my surprise, you announced, "I'm going to make love to my girlfriend. Do you want to watch or participate?"

With wide eyes and a Cheshire cat grin, Xander hopped off the bed. "I don't mind watching. I can join you if you want me to."

"Fine by me," you said as you gently pushed me onto the bed.

As I am dressed in nothing but a bath towel, you removed it to reveal my breasts. Moans of ecstasy escaped my lips with each nibble. Seductively, you gently kissed me from head to toe and back before you stripped yourself naked. Glancing over at Xander, you said, "I bet you don't know her secret spot."

Accepting your challenge, Xander crept over to the bed to kneel between my legs. After licking his middle finger, Xander swirled it around in my pussy. Within seconds, I came at his touch, squirting into his palm. Immediately, he pulled his finger out to eat me.

"Ooooh Daddy! YES! Right THERE!" I screamed.

"Hmmm, lemme see if I can find another spot," you said as you sucked on my nipples.

Fully enjoying the attention I am receiving from the both of you, I relaxed as you kissed me while Xander continued eating me.

"SWITCH!" you announced to let Xander know that you wanted to change places with him.

"No!" I snapped, taking control of the situation as I am ALWAYS in charge of my sexcapades. "It's time for us to pleasure *you*, Tracy."

Knowing what I had in mind, Xander undressed while I took off your clothes. Looking from me to Xander, I noticed your apprehension turned to excitement once you saw him in full naked view.

"Oh myyyyy!" you inhaled as you observed Xander stroking his dick to complete erection. While he strapped on a condom, I attacked your clit. "Ooooh Baby," you purred. "Lick that phat kat!"

"What did I tell you about giving me commands?" I said as I turned you to smack your ass.

"I'm sorry, Mama!" you said as you got up on all fours to pose in doggie position. Usually at this point, I strapped on a dildo but why bother when we have a real live specimen in our presence?

Taking my place behind you, Xander double checked the fit of the condom before slid into your moist walls.

"Ooooh," you moaned as I positioned myself to straddle in front of you.

"You like that?" I asked as I started rubbing my clit. You nodded your head to respond, grabbing my thighs to eat me.

As Xander slowly pumped inside your juicy walls, you swirled your tongue inside mine until I'm about to cum in your mouth. Feeling the need for some dick in me, I hopped out from under you and lay spread eagle while Xander disposed of the condom before going to work on me. Without hesitation, he accepted my invitation while you passionately kissed me.

During the threesome, my cell phone rang. Too excited from the afternoon's activities to allow for interruptions, I rolled over and hugged you and Xander closer to me. It will be hours later before I check my voicemail...

ME

Awakening in between you and Xander, I carefully pried myself from your loving death grip to go to the bathroom. Taking my cellphone to check my messages, I saw a familiar number in my missed call log.

"Ian?" I asked aloud. I looked back to make sure I hadn't woken either you or Xander with my exclamation before I continued walking into the master bathroom to take a shower.

Although my phone number had been the same with every upgrade, I hadn't heard from my ex-husband since the day our divorce became final.

Why is he calling me now?!

After turning on the shower's hot water to full blast, I sat on the toilet as I re-listened to the message. Getting wet at hearing his Smokey Robinson voice again after all these years, I exhaled as I pictured Ian Donovan nervously calling me.

"Hey Missy! Long time no hear from, huh? I'm just glad you never changed your number because I had no other way to reach you. My

number is still the same, too. Call me please? I…
I miss you, Missy."

"OK, Universe, what gives?" I said, looking
upward, flushing the toilet. "Tracy and Cynda
are getting along. I'm getting married to a man
that encourages my pansexuality so why on
Earth is my ex-prude coming back?!"

Stepping into the shower, I debated who I
would tell first: Xander, Tracy, or Cynda? My
future husband needed to know that my ex-
husband had reached out to me but so did my
girlfriends.

"Boo, can I join you?" you asked.

"If you have to ask…" I teased, welcoming
your interruption of my thoughts.

"You know I don't take *no* for an answer,"
you said as you entered the stall to stand behind
me.

With just enough room to stand, the most
you can do is kiss and finger me. Knowing you
try to make love to me everywhere we are, I had
already calculated the best angle to pleasure you
as Xander and I had made love in this shower
countless times before, specifically designed for
such occasions. Before I switched places to stand
behind you, you turned me around to face the
wall.

"Spread your legs," you commanded as you cupped my breasts to squeeze my nipples.

Growling, I looked back at you. "Tracy, what did I tell you about giving me commands?" I barked as I turned around to face you.

Pinching my clit, you whispered, "Want me to stop?"

"Mmmm…" I moaned.

You inched your fingers deeper into my pussy, spreading and flicking as you entered me.

"Ooooh…" I purred.

You knelt down on your knees to clamp your mouth onto my clit! As you began to repetitively tongue kiss me inside Kitten's mouth, I happily allow you to have your way with me.

"Dammit Baby!" I screamed as I grabbed your hair, urging you to go deeper, knowing your tongue can only go so far.

"Need some help?" Xander inquired with a devilish grin.

"Yes!" I exhaled, on the verge of cumming all over the shower. Xander tapped you on the shoulder as an indication for you two to switch places. Instead of eating me, Xander lifted me up and slid me onto his dick! Positioned securely in the custom-made shower stall, Xander ground his hips until his thickness was completely inside me, thrusting deeper and deeper. Gripping each other's shoulders, he whispered, "Mistress, do I please you?

"Oh Master, YES!!!" I screamed as I came all over Xander's manhood, still at attention.

Looking over at you, I am pleased to see you happily smiling back at me. The ringing of my cellphone on the bathroom counter startled us all. You read the caller ID aloud.

"Cynda."

As my longtime girlfriend's ringtone continued to play Katy Perry's "I Kissed A Girl", we all froze. You looked at me. Xander looked at me as he lowered me to the floor. I stared at the phone on the counter.

"Go ahead and take the call," Xander said with a kiss to my cheek. "I'm sure she'll be happy to hear your great news!"

Before I could step out of the shower, the ringtone stopped playing.

"I need to see her in person to tell her. Mind if I invite her over?" I asked you both.

"Fine with me," Xander smiled genuinely as you towel dried me.

"We can have a mini poly party! Mistress

and her Loves!" you cheered.

Xander and I looked at each other and laughed as we all exited the bathroom.

When Cynda arrived an hour later, I still hadn't found the words to explain Ian's return.

"Congratulations Mistress and Xander! Congratulations Mistress and Tracy! Welcome to the family, Xander and Tracy!" Cynda cheered as we all held up glasses of champagne to toast our polycule. "So should we set up a schedule or just go with Mistress' flow like we've been doing."

"The only thing that's gonna change is her last name," Xander said as he squeezed me to his side.

Looking up at my fiancé, I chuckled. "What makes you think I'm changing my name? Mistress Harding is just fine."

Frowning, Xander asked, "You don't want to be a Master?"

"Mistress Master?" Cynda sneered.

"Mistress Harding-Master?" you offered.

To halt further discussion, I gave my final answer: "Mistress Harding."

Kissing me, Xander said, "Yes ma'am."

"So where do y'all want to go celebrate? It's salsa night at *Meringue*!" Cynda announced with a quick Latin dance step.

Holding my hand up, I said, "Before we do any celebrating, I wanted you all to know that my ex-husband called me today. I haven't heard from him since the day our divorce became final and I haven't called him back but he left me this message."

As I played back Ian's voicemail, I watched and waited for my Loves' reactions.

"Hey Missy! Long time no hear from, huh? I'm just glad you never changed your number because I had no other way to reach you. My number is still the same, too. Call me please. I… I miss you, Missy."

"Damn, he still sounds SEXY!" Cynda swooned.

"Missy?" you queried.

"His pet name for me. He thought *Mistress* sounded so dirty. He always wanted me to be a nice traditional girl for him to marry and settle down with but he knew from the jump that there wasn't anything traditional about the things I did." Cutting a look at Cynda, I smirked.

"Invite him to the celebration," Xander suggested, stunning us all.

"Invite your fiancée's ex-husband to your engagement party?!" you exclaimed.

"Why not?" Xander replied seriously. "He knows she's polyamorous. If he thought that was just a phase she was going through, he can see for himself that we are all in her life and we all love her."

"What if he reacts poorly? Thinking he had a second chance only to find out YOU are the competition?" you exclaimed. "I'm just trying to prevent negative energy from being added to the festivities."

"One, Ian wouldn't fight over a woman. He would want her to be happy with someone else as long as she's honest with him," I explained.

"So he's poly now?!" Cynda asked in disbelief.

"No, I would say more of a cuckold from what my mother has told me. Over the years, every woman after me has cheated on him simply because he loves differently."

"And, two, love isn't a competition. I don't see a fight as long as she's still marrying me. If he loves her as she is and if she wants him back, Mistress can have Ian as her boyfriend," Xander added.

I couldn't love any of you any more than I did at that moment. Feeling the need to share my love, I group hugged my fiancé and girl-friends.

"But I feel ya on the bad vibes and we don't want that at our engagement party. Let's invite him over here tonight for a meet and greet," my fiancé suggested.

Perking up, I agreed. "Yes, that'll work. If that goes well, we can decide if we want to invite him to any future gatherings, For now, I want to see where his head is at. Like I said, I haven't heard from him since the day our divorce became final. Days before that, as he always did during our marriage, he called every day upon his arrival at work and every night to let me know he was home from work, especially after I moved into a hotel suite. His calls stopped the day our divorce became finalized."

Realizing how hurt I was by my first love's abrupt absence from my life, I comforted myself with knowing that we loved each other enough to let each other go to be happy with others.

"I'll call and see if he's available," I stated as everyone began preparing for our guest's arrival. Before I could dial his number, Ian was calling me!

Clearing my throat and letting out a deep exhale, I answered my phone. "Hello, Ian."

"Missy! Oh wow! Oh thank God this is still your number! I thought that I was having a wrong number moment and I didn't want to keep calling the wrong number because I really miss you and I was just hoping to have a drink with you and talk with you but I miss you, Missy!" Ian gushed once he confirmed that he had the right number. "Are you still there?!"

Chuckling, I replied, "Actually I was calling to invite you over to meet my family."

"Oh…" Ian sounded surprised then elated. "Oh! You had kids! Congratulations Missy! I always knew you would make a great mother! You have so much love to give! Tell me all about them!"

Suppressing a chortle, I said, "I'll do that when you come over. I'll text you the address. Come over anytime tonight after 7."

"Can't wait to see you again, Missy!" Ian exclaimed before ending the call.

Shaking her head, Cynda said, "He's in for quite the surprise when he meets your *family*!"

Rolling my eyes at my girlfriend, the ladies and I gave my fiancé a shopping list of food and drinks we would need before we retreated to the master bedroom to freshen up while Xander prepared appetizers. Once I was finished dressing myself in a purple, pink and blue floral print spaghetti strapped sundress, I entered the kitchen to relieve Xander of his duties and allowed him to get dressed before Ian's arrival.

"You! I love!" I said, imitating Yoda as I poked my head into the kitchen.

Xander turned to pick me up in his arms and kiss me. "You! I love! I'm gonna go and change before he gets here."

"Thank you for doing this," I said to Xander with a kiss. "This will either be a new beginning or complete closure. Either way, I'm happy I'm here with you."

With one last kiss, I scooted my fiancé away as I prepared my Super Nachos.

"By the time Ian gets here, those should be done," I smiled, sliding a baking tray of Cool Ranch Doritos chips and ground Angus with shredded Monterrey Jack and Colby cheese into the oven. Next, I mixed a batch of my Mistress-ritas, my own personal margarita concoction. Knowing that Ian was purely non-alcoholic, I had strawberry-peach-orange juice set aside just for him.

DING DONG!!

"Oooooh! Heeeee's heeeeere!" Cynda cheered.

Allowing Xander to open the door, I stood between you and Cynda. Immediately upon seeing my face, my former spouse smiled.

"Oh Missy!" They ignored everyone to rush forward and kiss me! "I've missed you so much!"

Clearing his throat, Xander closed the door.

Realizing that we weren't alone, our guest apologized. "Oh my goodness! Oh! I'm so... I'm so sorry! I... I... I just saw Missy and... My apologies!"

Chuckling with an extended hand, my fiancé said, "Hi, I'm Xander."

"And I'm Tracy," you chirped as you introduced yourself.

Waving her hand, Cynda grinned, "Hey Love! I'm loving your new look!!"

My first love only had eyes for me, once again neglecting the fact that we weren't alone to again kiss me full on my glossy lips. As we pulled away from our embrace, I began the introductions. "This is my fiancé Xander Master, my girlfriend Tracy Mills, and my girlfriend... Oh well you know Cynda. Everyone, this is..."

"Ianna Beaman, formerly Ian Donovan, the ex-husband."

I looked upon them with joy before looking from Xander to you to Cynda then back to our guest as you exclaimed, "Oh… Wow!"

To be continued in…

Mistress Harding Book 2: Cougar Mama

Excerpts from Mistress Harding Part 2…

Cougar Mama…

MISTRESS

When my mother named me Mistress, I'm sure she didn't expect me to take my moniker so seriously! I discovered early in life that I wasn't like the other girls. For one, I liked girls as much as I liked boys. Equally in fact. I didn't separate them by gender but instead by each individual themself. However, when I initially explored my sexual side, I started with the boys.

Ian Donovan was my first lover and my first love. Or so what I thought was love at the time. He was a doting boyfriend, always trying to keep a smile on my face by doing anything and everything I asked of him. Luckily for him, I wasn't as manipulative as a pre-teen as I later evolved to be as an adult. Losing our virginity to each other, I convinced him that ALL of his friends would enter junior high school with their cherries already popped.

"Don't you want me to be happy?" I asked on our last day of grade school. "Next year, we start junior high school. We'll have all summer to get it right so that by the time we start next year, we'll be pros!"

"Of course I want you to be happy, Missy. But shouldn't we wait until we get married to have sex?" asked Ian. Born and raised by very religious parents, most of Ian's family believed in following the rules of the Bible. I wasn't raised that way. My marital role models were non-existent and the idea of monogamy was never enforced as evidenced by the fact that my mother and father each had separate relation-ships outside their union.

"What if I don't want to get married?" I asked seriously. We were only 13 years old and this boy was thinking about MARRIAGE?!

"Why do you want to have sex if you don't want to get married?" Ian inquired.

I simply looked at him. "You don't have to be married to have sex."

"Yes, you do!" he exclaimed. "Mama says that I can't have sex until I get married."

Sauntering over to my boyfriend, I said, "Ian, is your sister married?"

Looking shamefaced, he replied, "No... but..."

"And yet..." I paused long enough for Ian and I to hear the panting coming from the Donovan's basement. Ian's older sister, Qiana, was getting her freak on with her own boyfriend, making me jealous.

"Well, Key doesn't want to get married but I do!" declared Ian.

With exasperation, I looked at him. "I guess we should break up now then because I'm not getting married. Not just to have sex."

I barely took two steps toward the front door before Ian grabbed my hand.

"Missy, I know we're too young for marriage, but aren't we too young for sex?" he asked.

"I'm ready. If *you're* not, then YOU aren't old enough. Haven't you been having funny feelings down here?" I ask as I grab his penis. Instantly, he grew harder.

"Y-y-yeah but..." he stuttered.

Softly kissing his neck and ears, I said, "You can't get married for at least another six years. You really wanna feel like this..." Gently, I squeezed his dick for emphasis. "For... six... years...?" I continued kissing Ian until our lips met.

"Oh, Missy... I wanna but..." Ian's hesitation was beginning to piss me off. Since he was my boyfriend, he had first dibs on breaking me in but little did he know, others were waiting in line to take his place! No time like the present to lay all my cards on the table.

Knowing how Ian felt about me, I felt a tad apologetic for being so devious but I also didn't want to waste anyone's time, mine or Ian's. "Look, you don't have to do this with me. I'll find someone else. But of course, I don't want to cheat on you so that means we'll have to break up first."

"Break up?! No, Missy!!! I… I… I'll do it!" he agreed, half-heartedly.

At that point, sex was purely physical for me. After we snuck a condom out of his sister's room, Ian and I went back to his bedroom to have sex for the first time ever. Going simply from my father's pornos, I thought I had an idea of what to do. I knew Ian's penis would enter my vagina, he would pump a few times, I would scream "Oh baby" or something like that, show's over.

It didn't go quite like that.

Ian nervously took his clothes off a piece at a time while I exuberantly stripped naked and jumped into his bed. His parents would be home in a couple of hours and who knew how much longer his sister would be fucking in the basement so we didn't have much time to use or lose.

"Come on, Baby," I urged Ian. His hands were shaking as he attempted to open the condom wrapper. Taking it from him in my frustration, I ripped it open and slid the condom on Ian. Pulling him into the bed on top of me, I opened my legs so that he could enter me. Poor Ian had NO clue what to do! I was the only one who was ready! As I looked down, his penis was losing power so I quickly grabbed it, much to Ian's surprise.

"Oh, Missy!" he said as he grew harder while I guided him toward my clit. Once he was inside, he moaned. "Damn! Is it supposed to be this tight?"

Giggling, I said, "Just the first few times, until you get used to it."

Hell, I didn't know he would be as big as he was so I prayed to God that he COULD get back in there!

Once he got his rhythm, Ian had me gripping sheets and covering my mouth, praying no one would hear us!

"Damn, Missy, you feel so goooood!" he panted.

"Oh, Baby!" I exhaled as I wrapped my legs around his waist.

When we heard the footsteps of his sister

approaching, we halted our movement until…

KNOCK! KNOCK! KNOCK!

Gripping me close to him, his penis still firmly positioned deep inside my walls, Ian waited a moment before responding.

"Yeah?!" he said with annoyance.

"Y'all ah'ight in there?" Qiana asked with a giggle.

Something told me she knew what we were doing. Were we THAT loud??

"Yeah, we're good!" Ian snapped back, ready to get back to the action.

"Lemme know if y'all need another condom!" Qiana laughed out loud. "Mom and Dad called. They'll be home late so take your time!"

Continuing on with our mission, Ian looked down at me and smiled before continuing to make love to me.

After a year of heterosexual intercourse, I discovered that I wanted and needed more than what Ian could offer. My attraction toward girls increased after I lost my virginity to him. Now I wanted to see what it was like to have sex with a girl! However, knowing that my feelings weren't like everyone else's, I couldn't just walk up to a girl and say "Hey, I like you. Wanna fuck?" Luckily for me, I confided in my best friend, Cynda.

"You like girls, too?" she asked incredulously as we sat in my bedroom. "Aren't you dating Ian Donovan?"

"Yeah but he doesn't have what girls have. I want to see what sex is like with a girl," I admitted.

"Wish I could help you," Cynda said quietly.

Grinning, I said, "Maybe you can."

Looking up at me, Cynda looked ashen. "I... I don't think so. I'm..."

"You're not into girls?" I asked dejectedly.

"Actually, I am. In fact, there's just one girl that I want," said Cynda, bashfully.

Intrigued, I said, "Oh, really? Do I know her?"

Chuckling, Cynda said, "Yeah..."

Knowing she was talking about me, I gently placed my hand on Cynda's thigh but she quickly jumped away from me. "I'm sorry," I apologized, expressing regret for being so forward with my best friend.

"No! No, I'm sorry," she said, reaching for me. "Missy, there's something I need to tell you."

Pulling her to the bed to sit next to me, I said, "What is it, Cyn?"

Almost in a whisper, Cynda said, "I'm... I'm a lesbian.

In confusion, I parroted, "Lesbian?"

"I've never had any attraction to boys," she admitted.

Intrigued, I said, "Really?"

She simply nodded her head.

"I won't tell anyone. I promise," I admitted.

Cynda and I had been best friends since 2nd grade. Thick as thieves, if you saw her, you saw me. Until now, we had no reason to see each other completely naked. Now I really wanted to!

Slowly, she stood up to pull down her shorts and panties. In amazement, I reached for her. "Wow..."

Stepping back, Cynda looked embarrassed.

"No, Baby. Come here," I urged, tugging Cynda to sit on the bed. Parting her legs, I knelt in front of her. "I don't know where to begin!" Not waiting for a suggestion, I fingered her pussy with my left hand. When I felt a tingling between my own legs, I gently kissed her pussy with my mouth. Assuming this was

Cynda's first time having sex with anyone, I was privileged to be the first to eat her out!

"Oh my GOD!" she panted as I slid more fingers inside her. "I never thought... I never believed..."

Kissing her passionately, I said, "Just enjoy it, Baby!"

When it felt like Cynda was about to cum inside my mouth, I leapt off of her! Looking over at Cynda, I smiled briefly before I thought about Ian.

"Fuck!" I exclaimed.

Rising up on her elbow, Cynda looked at me. "What's wrong, Missy?"

Sitting up and putting my head in my hands, I said, "I just cheated on Ian!"

"Oh no! I... I didn't..." Cynda stammered.

Shushing her, I said, "No, Baby. I wanted you and I wanted to do this. It was in the heat of the moment and I didn't want to let this opportunity pass by."

"I don't want you to be unfaithful, Missy," said Cynda. "It'll just be this one time."

Saddened, I said, "Is that what *you* want?"

"No! I want YOU but you're already with someone," Cynda stated.

Looking surprised, I stared at Cynda. "You

want me?"

Sheepishly, she grinned. "Of course I do! You're my best friend, Missy! I told you my secret and instead of running away, you made love to me!"

Sex with Cynda was amazing! I didn't want to let her go but I didn't want to lose Ian either!

"Who says I have to be with just one person?!" I snapped.

Sounding confused, Cynda asked, "So what are you saying?"

"I have a boyfriend and a girlfriend!" I declared.

Looking shocked, Cynda said, "Girlfriend?"

Taking Cynda's hands into mine, I said, "Baby, you and I are a unique couple. We may never find anyone else like us. If you want to explore with other people, as long as you don't hurt me or us, go have your fun and I'll do the same."

"We can't..." she began.

Kissing her, I said, "Do you want me?"

"Yes! Yes I do!" she exclaimed.

"Then as long as you want me, I'm yours," I said with another kiss. "And I'll understand if you want to keep this on the low."

Looking down, Cynda said, "I want to tell

the world you're mine but I don't want anyone to hurt us. And what about Ian?"

"I'll deal with him," I said as a thought came to my mind. "Have you ever had sex with a boy?"

Shaking her head, Cynda admitted, "You are the only person I've ever had sex with."

Pleased with the honor of being her first, I asked, "Would you want to?"

"I… I don't know…" she said hesitantly. "I mean, I just don't find them sexually attractive. No, I would rather give my all to just one person."

Torn between two lovers, not wanting to lose either, I agreed to continue my relationship with my boyfriend while keeping my girlfriend behind closed doors.

IAN

I don't think a day will ever come when I will stop loving my Missy. She was my first for so many of my life's major events. She was my first girlfriend. My first lover. My first wife. My first love. She was everything I thought I ever needed.

But unfortunately, I wasn't enough for her.

I learned soon after we first had sex that she needed more than I could give her when she confessed that she was attracted to girls. I was devastated when she revealed that she had slept with her best friend Cynda. Not wanting anyone else to have the pleasure she gave me, going so far as to skip school just to see her, I did everything I could to keep Missy satisfied but my grades began to slip and my parents threatened to send me to military school if I didn't break up with her. I could never let Missy go! I loved her so much that I went against my parents' wishes and had premarital sex with her!

Dating from junior high to college, I felt secure in my belief that our marriage would last forever as I proposed on graduation day. But I couldn't keep up with Missy's growing sexual appetite.

"Ian, I love you but... I need more and I can't have that if I'm married to you," she explained.

"You have Cynda and me. What more do you need?" I inquired.

"Freedom to do what I want. Marriage doesn't allow that," she stated.

"Our marriage will be whatever we want it to be. I'll do whatever you want to keep you happy. Just say yes!" I implored.

It took me over a year to convince Missy to marry me. That should've been my hint that we wouldn't work. I shouldn't've had to profusely persuade her to share my life with me but I wanted Missy so badly! My only lover, she was everything I needed in the bedroom. She studied sex like she was getting a Master's degree in it! Constantly coming up with new ways to pleasure me, I was always satisfied. Since her only complaint was that she wanted to include a girl in our sexcapades, against my better judgment, I agreed to a threesome.

"I assume you want to invite Cynda," I said after I reluctantly agreed.

"No, I want someone new," Missy stated.

New?

"Why do you want someone new?" I inquired, assuming she would want her usual female partner to join us.

"Cynda won't have sex with you, Ian," Missy explained.

"You already asked her?!" I exclaimed, pissed that she had invited her girlfriend into a threesome before she knew if I wanted to participate.

"She doesn't sleep with men," Missy said matter-of-factly.

"Damn! Well, I guess that's fine. So how do we find someone new?" I asked, fearful that Missy had already found a woman.

"If you like, I can find her. I'm sure you don't want to include a man, right?" Missy asked, looking directly into my eyes.

"No! Of course not!" I exclaimed. "You know I'm not gay!"

Looking perturbed, Missy frowned. "You didn't have to say it like *that*, Ian."

Feeling guilty for my tone and words, I apologized. "Baby, I'm sorry. You know I don't have anything against gay people."

"I should hope not since your wife is bisexual," she stated with an edge to her voice.

"Exactly…" I replied. "Do you already have someone in mind or can we find her together?"

"Both," Missy replied as she proceeded to strip naked before me.

Immediately, my dick stood at attention at the sight of my beautiful wife's toned body. Years of running kept her 5'8" frame in top condition.

"If you don't like Rissa, we can search for someone else," my wife explained as she sauntered into our master bathroom.

"Rissa?" Well, her name is pretty. And as picky as my Missy is, I'm sure she's gorgeous. "Where and how did you meet her?" I asked as I undressed to join my wife in the shower.

"She caught me while I was running," Missy said as I joined her in the bathroom. "She was in the bleachers just watching me run around the track. I noticed she would be in the stands every once in a while until she was there every time I was. One day, I approached her and we began talking."

"Interesting…" I said as we entered the large shower built especially for the two of us. "So she was checking you out, just waiting for you to notice her?"

"Yes," said Missy as she stood behind me,

soaping my back with a washcloth and body wash. "I walked up to her and asked her point blank if she was stalking me."

Laughing as I turned to face Missy, I said, "Well, that's definitely a memorable introduction!"

Grinning, she replied, "You know me, Ian. Live and direct."

"True! Well, obviously you didn't scare her away with that statement or the fact that you're married." Nervously, I wondered, did she tell Rissa that she was married??

"Actually, she seemed more interested in me when I mentioned you," said Missy as she turned around to let me soap her back. "And no, I didn't ask her about a threesome. She and I are still at the getting to know you stage."

"When did you meet her?" I asked with renewed interest.

"Officially, a couple of weeks ago. She's been *stalking* me for about a month though." Once we'd rinsed ourselves off and exited the bathroom, Missy continued the conversation. "I showed her our wedding picture. She thinks you're sexy."

Blushing, I replied, "Cool! So what does she look like?"

Retrieving her cellphone from her nightstand, Missy searched through her photos. "Here she is."

My wife showed me a picture of the second most gorgeous woman I had ever laid my eyes on, my wife of course being the first. Missy had a few pictures of Rissa by herself as well as a selfie they took together. Curves and thickness in all the right places, she looked like a fuller caramel version of Missy.

"Wow!" was all I could say. THIS was the woman my wife wanted us to have a threesome with?! "Hell yeah I'm in!!"

I co-signed too soon. With the hopes that allowing my wife the opportunity to get her rocks off with me and another lover would strengthen our marriage, I assumed Missy would be satisfied. Instead, her sexual appetite only INCREASED!! Although she always gave me the first right of refusal, she still pissed me off when I would decline because she would simply go to Cynda or Rissa for release.

"At least it's not another man," I said to console myself.

From the moment after our threesome with

Rissa, it was a matter of time before Missy would become bored with me. Working long hours to give her the life I believed my wife deserved kept me away from her more than either of us anticipated. With the extra hours I was putting in, I would come home so exhausted that I could barely enjoy the nightly or morning blowjobs Missy attempted to give me.

Within a year after our one and only threesome, Missy filed for divorce. Knowing that I could never fully satisfy my wife, I signed the papers and gave her back her freedom.

CYNDA

"I'm never letting you do *that* again!" I declared as Missy and I celebrated the demise of her marriage. "And look! You're already starting to perk up! I can't believe how much of an anchor that man was on you!" I could see that Missy was holding back her tears. Hugging her close to me, I said, "I know you loved Ian. I'm sorry for being insensitive."

Shaking her head as she wiped her tears away, Missy said, "Well now that *that's* over, what's next?"

One thing I loved about my Missy was the fact that she never let a bad mood stay with her for too long. My Baby was always the bright spot in my days and although I was prepared to pamper her until she felt better, she seemed to be handling her divorce in stride.

"On to the next one!" she declared to my astonishment.

"*Next*?! You want to get married *again*?!" I asked in disbelief.

"Fuck no!" Missy exclaimed to my relief. "But you know I need at least one penis in my roster and since I only deal with one at a time, I have to replace Ian."

"Oh…" I said dejectedly.

"Baby! No! Now *I'm* being insensitive! No offense to you at all! You know I need you, too!" Missy apologized.

Taking a deep breath, I chose my words carefully. "Missy, maybe you should take some time and be by yourself for a while. Reconnect with you before you bring more male energy into your life."

Nodding in agreement, Missy replied, "You're right, Cyn. I really need to recover from this. I tried so hard to fight my denial but I knew all along that I never should've tied myself down to one person, male or female. I'm too independent to have someone fully depending on me. Or worse, I can't depend on them!"

Half-heartedly, I agreed. Missy was always trying to do things without me or Ian around to know what she was up to. Although I trusted that Missy was being careful, I always worried about her.

Now that I had the opportunity to have Missy all to myself for a while, I invited her to move in with me. "Just until you get back on your feet," I suggested. Thankfully, Missy agreed.

The next five years flew by as my girl-friend and I used up all of our vacation time to travel together. An extended weekend in Cozumel. A week in Rome. A cruise to Alaska. Nearly a month in Sydney, Australia. The flex-ibility of our schedules as well as my family's many business connections allowed Missy and me to stay for free pretty much wherever we landed. An openly polyamorous couple, we always made an impression wherever we went, flirting with every beautiful woman and hand-some man that came within our line of sight. Watching Missy in action was both pleasurable and painful for me. Not necessarily comfortable with men around, I would allow her to be alone with her male company yet I wanted to be in on the action whenever a woman was involved.

On one rare occasion when Missy and I didn't have plans together, I went out to the movies without her. Missy was in an unusual funk that I just couldn't pull her out of and she insisted on being left alone. Reluctantly, I treated myself to a matinee and a light lunch. After my movie and as I waited for my meal, I called to check on Missy but my calls went directly to voicemail. In an effort to not worry about her, I dismissed her from my mind and focused on staying positive. Whenever I worried about Missy, I ended up in physical pain (stomach aches and migraines) only to find out that she was perfectly safe and sound the entire time we were apart.

"Is this seat taken?"

Looking up, I was pleasantly surprised to lay my eyes on a stunningly attractive woman. She was staring intently at me, awaiting my response.

"Uh… no! No, it's not. Would you like to join me?" I offered politely, gesturing toward the nearest empty chair at my table.

Hypnotized by the thickness of her hips, I couldn't help staring as she descended into an available seat. Extending her hand toward me, she said, "Hi, I'm Tracy."

Beaming back at her, I introduced myself. "Cynda."

"A beautiful name for a beautiful woman," said Tracy.

Blushing at the compliment, I thanked her as I looked around the café. Although there were plenty of empty tables, I was pleased that Tracy decided to join me at mine. "May I ask why you're alone?"

Smirking, Tracy replied, "I didn't think you would say hello if I had an entourage with me."

Taken aback, I said, "Huh?"

"This is one of my favorite places to relax and I've seen you come in from time to time, usually alone. Every once in a while with a beautiful woman but generally alone," stated Tracy. "I've wanted to introduce myself on several occasions and this was the first time I got up the nerve to do it."

"Oh!" I expressed with genuine surprise. "Wow! I'm flattered." Realizing Tracy had seen me with Missy, I felt obligated to "introduce" her as well. "The woman you've seen me with is my girlfriend, Missy. She didn't feel well and told me to go out and enjoy myself."

"Are you doing as you were told?" Tracy smiled at me.

Grinning, I said, "Yes, ma'am."

Cringing, Tracy asked, "Can I please not be referred to as *ma'am*? I'm not even 30 yet!"

"Oh baby, I'm sorry! I didn't mean to offend

you," I immediately apologized.

Patting my hand, Tracy chuckled. "You are so sweet. No need to apologize. I was just teasing you." After a moment of silence allowed my nerves to settle, she began with the interrogation.

"So Missy wasn't feeling well tonight? I'm sorry to hear that," Tracy commented.

A bit perturbed that Tracy was so quickly comfortable talking about my girlfriend as if she knew her, I changed the subject.

"Dumb question but I'm going to ask. Are you into women?" I inquired.

Smiling broadly, Tracy replied, "Very much so! I came out as bisexual when I was 15. Still looking forward to my first girlfriend though. I never have an issue talking to men but I'm too shy to meet women."

A part of me tensed up although I knew nothing of my outward appearance could give away my secret. I always dressed as femininely as I could to avoid any awkward questions. However, Tracy's ease of talking to me after she confessed to being shy about meeting women put me on edge.

"As gorgeous as you are, I would think women would be knocking each other down just to get to you!" I said truthfully.

"Hell! I *wish*!" Tracy laughed out loud. "I generally clam up around women, especially the most beautiful ones!"

When Tracy began humming bars from the Prince and the Revolution's song of the same name, I was thankful the moment was silenced by Missy's ringtone.

"Excuse me. This is Missy," I said, excusing myself from my table. Once I was out of Tracy's earshot, I took my girlfriend's call. "Hey Baby! How YOU doin?"

"Sorry I've missed your calls, Love. I just woke up when Rissa called," she explained.

Rissa?! What the fuck?! You couldn't hear my *ringtone but you heard* hers*?!*

"Do you mind if she stops by for a visit?" Missy asked, interrupting my pissed off thoughts.

"I'm on my way home," I said as I stomped back to my table to pay my bill. Tracy was still there, patiently waiting for my return only to watch me walk out of the café without a goodbye.

"No need to cut your evening short, Cyn. I was just letting you know I'm having a guest over."

"Which is it, Missy? Are you asking me if she can come over or are you telling me she's already there?!" I snapped as I unlocked my car.

"I don't like your tone, Cynda," Missy replied calmly. "I'll see you when you come home."

Click.

Never one to say goodbye at the end of a phone call, I wasn't surprised at the abrupt ending. It was what Missy said and how she said it that disturbed me.

I don't like your tone, Cynda.

"Here I go again. Either I trust Missy or I don't!" I warned myself as I pulled onto our street. Not a single vehicle left our apartment complex so that told me either Rissa was already gone, still at our place, or she never showed up. I was praying for the latter as I sat in my car for a few extra minutes. Gathering my courage, I rode the elevator to the 15th floor. As I approached our apartment, I prayed I found Missy alone and happy to see me.

Quietly, I opened the door to see Missy curled up on the couch reading a book. Relieved to see that my girlfriend was home alone, I walked over to her to kiss her hello.

"Did you enjoy your evening?" she said

with a pleasant tone.

Surprised, I replied honestly, "I did until you called me."

Furrowing her brow, Missy looked up from her book to stare at me. "What changed your mood?"

"What you said and how you said it," I stated, sitting in the chair across from the sofa.

"What did I say that upset you, Cyn?" Missy asked as she patted the couch cushion next to her.

"You said 'I don't like your tone, Cynda,' as if I didn't have the right to ask my questions. You are my girlfriend and I have a right to know who's in our home while I'm away. Not just for the security of our home but also for the safety of my girlfriend," I explained, walking over to join Missy on the couch.

Shifting to face me, Missy said, "Cynda, have I ever cheated on you?"

Taken aback by the question, I snapped, "Hell no!"

"So why would I start *now*? I'm polyamorous. Honesty, non-possessiveness, and transparency are paramount to me in *all* of my relationships. I called to let you know that I might have a guest coming over. If I were cheating, you wouldn't've gotten *any* calls," she revealed.

After taking a deep breath, I slowly exhaled. "Baby, I'm sorry. You're right. You've always been honest and upfront with me. I've never had a reason to doubt you and I won't start now."

"Good to hear," Missy said before kissing me. "So, until I called, you were enjoying yourself?"

Smiling to myself, I thought about Tracy. "I met a young lady tonight."

Perking up, Missy took my hands into hers. "Tell me all about her! How old is she? Does she have any kids? How cute is she?"

Missy seemed to be more interested in Tracy than I was but that was probably because she was usually the one answering these kinds of questions from me.

"Well, as it turns out, she's been checking me out for a while," I confessed. "She said she comes into the café regularly and has seen me there a few times, sometimes with you. Since I was alone tonight, she was brave enough to introduce herself."

"Interesting… And what's her name?" Missy asked.

"Tracy," I replied with a grin as I envisioned the beautiful young woman that expressed an interest in me. "I didn't ask but I believe she's in her mid to late 20's since she said she's not even 30 yet. I don't think she has any children but we didn't get that deep into the conversation. She's cute, thick and flirty."

Nodding in approval, Missy asked, "Did y'all exchange numbers and plan to meet again?"

Dropping my head, I said, "No. I left her while I was on the phone with you, thinking that you were up to something."

Looking at me with disappointment, Missy said, "I wish I could say that I understand why you felt that way but I don't. And to be honest, I'm offended that you would automatically assume I'm being devious when I have never given you a reason to doubt me. In fact, your accusation is making me look at *you*!"

Stunned by the inference, I defended myself. "Missy, I have *never* cheated on you and I have no reason to! You are all the woman that I need!"

"Is that right?" Missy asked as she sat back with her arms crossed over her chest.

"Yes!" I exclaimed.

"So maybe you were feeling guilty about talking to Tracy when I called and you assumed that I was up to something?" Missy hinted.

Thinking over my reaction to Missy's call while I was with Tracy, I realized that Missy was right. Although I was simply talking with Tracy, a part of me felt like I was cheating on Missy. I had planned on telling her about Tracy when I came home anyway because I've never had to hide anything from my girlfriend before and I wasn't about to start lying to her now!

"I guess I *was* feeling guilty. You know I'm not looking for anyone and rarely does anyone approach me unless you're with me so I was on edge the whole time!" I admitted.

Rubbing my hand, Missy said, "Awww, my sexy Baby didn't know she was a catch?!"

Blushing, I said, "You're the only woman I want to catch me."

"I already did that!" Missy said with a kiss. "And if you want to date other women, you know I am more than fine with that."

"Eh... we'll see. I think you would like Tracy though. Maybe she would like to have fun with us," I hinted, knowing how much fun it would be to watch Missy playing with Tracy.

"Hmmm... it's been a long time since I've

had a threesome. Get to know her better and see if that's where she's headed. Otherwise, you're more than welcome to enjoy her all alone," Missy offered.

Not once had I considered the idea of being with anyone but Missy. With her, I didn't have the questions or confused disgusted looks. She's loved me as I am since day one.

"Like I said, I think you'll like her. I'm not even gonna walk her down that path with me," I said, squeezing Missy close to me. "If we get closer and I get brave enough to tell her, then we'll see about that threesome. In the meantime, may *I* satisfy you?"

Kissing me softly, Missy replied, "Yes, you may!"

Taking her hands into mine, I led my lover into our bedroom.

To be continued in...

Mistress Harding Book 2: Cougar Mama

Meet The SistaGirlz

SistaGirlz: an Urban Fairy Tale book series contains strong language, graphic sexual content, and is intended for **MATURE READERS ONLY (ages 18 and older)**

In 2003 and 2004, I published my first two books, "Livin' Just Enough" (2003) and "Illusions" (2004). In 2010, I wrote a short story called "Neva Saw It Comin'" which was featured in Red Bud Ave. Publication's "Tales From The Lou", short stories written by four St. Louis authors. After a brief hiatus, I returned to my *first two books and my short story* and decided to continue writing by making a series out of the characters' personal stories. There are nine women in my **SistaGirlz** series: Rachael Wallace, Layla Michaels, Raven Powers, Imani Powers, TaMeeka James, Angela DeVille, Nina DeVille, JaShel Jackson, and Clarissa Revelin.

When I was in college, one of my professors

encouraged us to write what we know. At that time, I knew that I loved writing, my husband and children, traveling, shopping, going to the movies, dining out, hanging with my friends, sharing positivity, LOVE, and being polyamorous.

Now when I say I love LOVE, I mean the full **physical mental emotional spiritual** energy mix that I share with my Loves. Sex can be a physical release of tension and stress but the LOVE I share with my Loves gives me renewed strength to keep pushing forward in this thing called Life.

And polyamory? Well, whether my parents knew it or not, I was conceived polyamorously. My parents were ethically non-monogamous. Daddy was married with a child when he met and fell in love with Mama. He proposed to her several times but he was already married; she said no because that would make him a bigamist. He successfully supported both households for years. He stayed married until his death. My mother knew about his wife and children (one child born a few years before me, a child born a year before and one child born a year after me) and she still loved him. His wife knew about my mother and me yet she still loved him. I wasn't a secret love child. Because he had his wife's consent to continue his relationship with my mother, Daddy and his wife were polyamorous. Because my mother consented to continue a romantic relationship with my married father, she was polyamorous. Therefore, I was CONCEIVED AND BORN polyamorous! Which definitely comes in handy considering I'm pansexual. (Insert cheesy grin)

By writing this series, it is my goal to help share my love of ethical non-monogamy and help educate others about various non-monogamous lifestyles. My **SistaGirlz** are a reflection of different key points in *my* life. However, **SistaGirlz: an Urban Fairy Tale book series** is a work of fiction. All names, characters, and incidents portrayed in this production are fictitious. No identification with actual persons (living or deceased), places, buildings, and products is intended or should be inferred. To be clear, this is my fictionalized semi autobiography.

With that being said…

Do you know my Girlz?

Are you Monogamous

Non-monogamous

or Polyamorous?

- Cheater/Unethically Non-Monogamous = selfish non-monogamous liar
- Ethically Non-monogamous = many loves, no sexual/emotional exclusivity, 100% transparency
- Monogamous = ONE LOVE
- Non-monogamous = prefers many loves, may or may not be transparent
- Polyamorous = may have two or more lovers (male and/or female) with 100% transparency
- Polyandrous = prefers many male lovers
- Polygynous = prefers many female lovers

Some people only want to be with one person. Some people want to be with many lovers but they don't want anyone in their business.

And there are some people that want to be with many lovers that are aware of each other's presence, no lies or secrets.

Based on their Loves, which **SistaGirlz** are monogamous vs. non-monogamous? And if they're non-monogamous, are they cheaters, ethically non-monogamous, or polyamorous?

FYI there are many different non-monogamous titles. These are the main ones I'll be using.

Warning: reading further may spoil some of your enjoyment of reading the SistaGirlz series, already knowing what you'll learn about each character in another character's book. If you want to skip the spoilers, feel free to go to the next section. Otherwise, ENJOY!

The Men of SistaGirlz

As you read the series, you'll discover that the **SistaGirlz** identify as either Monogamous, Polyamorous or Ethically Non-monogamous.

However, their Loves may not necessarily "match".

Rachael (*Polyamorous*) loves Aaron (*Cheater turned Ethically Non-monogamous*) and Alonzo (*Monogamous*) in…
SistaGirlz Book 1
Livin' Just Enough
Rachael's Story
In 2003, I wrote a book called **LIVIN' JUST ENOUGH** with the story centered mainly around Rachael "Baby Girl" Wallace. She starts off with her childhood boyfriend Aaron Jones until he dumps her. Free to move on with her life, Rachael falls for Alonzo Banks but then Aaron comes back. What's a SistaGirl to do?

The *What He Did For Her Love* edition of **Livin' Just Enough** allows my readers to see what Aaron and Alonzo did to win Rachael's heart.

Layla (*Monogamous*) loves Nicolas (*Monogamous*) in…
SistaGirlz Book 2

Illusions
Layla's Story
In 2004, I wrote **LJE's** follow up, **ILLU-SIONS**. From this point forward, we see the story from more than just the main character's point of view. We begin as Layla Michaels meets and gets involved with handsome Nicolas Hayes much to the dismay of Layla's twin sister Kayla.

Raven (*Monogamous*) loves Randy (**CHEATER**) and Brian (*Monogamous*)
and
Imani (*Polyamorous*) loves Vincent (*Polyamorous*) in...
SistaGirlz Book 3
Neva Saw It Comin'
Raven & Imani's Story
In **NEVA SAW IT COMIN'**, we are introduced to twins Raven and Imani Powers. Similar in their love troubles but different as night and day, Raven and Imani keep each other grounded during the storms of their love lives.

Meeka (*Monogamous*) loves Darius (*Polyamorous*) and Chico (*Ethically Non-monogamous*) in...
SistaGirlz Book 4
Unexpected Detours
Meeka's Story
TaMeeka James' life hasn't been the easiest but she'll be the first to admit the part she played in it. Happily married to Chico Banks, TaMeeka thinks life can't get any sweeter until the return of her son's father, Darius Price proves otherwise. With unfinished business left on the table, Darius makes it his mission to reunite his family.

Angela (*Polyamorous*) loves Darius (*Polyamorous*), Devin (*Polyamorous*) and Aaron (*Ethically Non-monogamous*) in...
SistaGirlz Book 5
Unforgivable
Angela's Story
Past decisions come back to haunt Angela DeVille when she runs into her ex-high school sweetheart, Devin Lawson, who was unaware of her pregnancy when they parted ways. Reunited years later, this single mother has to

decide if telling the truth will set her free or do more harm than good.

Nina (*Ethically Non-monogamous*) loves Yusuf (*Cheater turned Ethically Non-monogamous*) in...
SistaGirlz Book 6
Her Ideal Husband
Nina's Story
Fun loving and free spirited Nina DeVille was the LAST of the **SistaGirlz** to WANT to settle down. Hypnotized by the aloofness of her non-committal lover Yusuf, Nina has to decide if "shacking up" is really the way she wants to live her life.

JaShel (*Polyamorous*) loves Jayson (**CHEATER** turned *Ethically Non-monogamous*), Antonio (*Monogamous*), and Xavier (*Polyamorous*) in...
SistaGirlz Book 7
JaShel's Trilogy
PART 1 THE FAITHFUL CHEATER
PART 2 BEHIND CLOSED DOORS
PART 3 WIFEY

By the time the dust settles on Part 3, JaShel Jackson has been married, knocked up 3 times, been cheated on, divorced, married, knocked up 4 mo' times, beaten on, and divorced. With 2 ex-husbands and 7 kids under her belt, JaShel was content to live her life taking care of her children, preferably without the never-ending pleas for reconciliation from both Jayson Clark and Antonio Black!

Clarissa (*Ethically Non-monogamous*) loves Franklin (*Ethically Non-monogamous*), Sam (*Ethically Non-monogamous*), and Mistress (*Ethically Non-monogamous*) in…
SistaGirlz Book 8
Clarissa's Trilogy
PART 1 HER LAST SEVEN DEADLY SINFUL DAYS
PART 2 SHE'S A HARD HABIT TO BREAK
PART 3 HER LAST FIRST KISS
Raised by her single father, Clarissa Revelin lived her life as she pleased, never taking anybody's bullshit and calling them on it when necessary. The only man she ever truly loved unknowingly shaped the future of her sex life.

Never falling for the "L" word, Clarissa enjoyed the pleasures her lovers showered upon her. Could anyone penetrate her rules to tame her heart?

SistaGirlz Book 9
SISTAGIRLZ FINALE...?

The lives of the **SistaGirlz** converge in the final(?) book in this entertaining, engaging, and thought provoking urban fairy tale series. Will marriages survive the truth? Who's the biggest surprise at the Banks Family Reunion? Who meets their demise?! Dirty laundry is aired left and right as old secrets come creeping out of the woodwork. Will their love for each other hold the **SistaGirlz** together or will revealed lies and betrayal separate them all forever?!

Please use **#SistaGirlzUrbanFairyTale**, **#DoYouKnowMyGirlz**, **#NoSecretsNoLies**, and **#MonogamyMeetsPolyamory** on Facebook, Instagram, and Twitter to help me spread the word about my **SistaGirlz**!

For more about Author Lea Mishell, find her on Facebook AuthorLeaMishell, follow her on Instagram @AuthorLeaMishell and Twitter @SistaGirlzBooks and help bring the **Sista-Girlz** to paperback

Stay tuned for details and release dates or go directly to Leanpub to purchase all of my available **SistaGirlz** e-book titles!!

I am aware that Books 1 and 2 were available on Amazon but those are OUTDATED VERSIONS!! DO NOT BUY MY BOOKS FROM AMAZON IF THEY DON'T SAY "SISTAGIRLZ". Thank you.

To learn more about Author Lea Mishell, check her out at https://about.me/leamishellink

PeaceLoveHappinessPolyamory
Lm…

Excerpt from Neva Saw It Comin'

SistaGirlz Book #3 Raven & Imani's Story

What happened to Rachael's mother? Will Kayla come back and stir up more trouble? Will Raven and Imani find luck in their love lives? Read **NEVA SAW IT COMIN'** to find out what happens next to the SistaGirlz!

"I wish I could find *one* faithful man!" my sister Imani lamented as she sulked in the passenger seat of my 2008 Chevy TrailBlazer. Just moments before, she and I caught her boyfriend, Vincent Wheeler, at his apartment with another woman between his legs.

"Damn *that*!" I nearly screamed as I started the ignition. "*No* woman should go through this hell! I wish any man that cheats on *me* drops dead in the other woman's pussy!"

I smirked as I saw Vincent's half naked body in my rearview mirror as he shouted Imani's name. Just as Vincent was joined by his female companion, I yelled out the window as I peeled out of the parking lot.

"Watch your back cuz if I *ever* see you around my sister, *I'll fuck you up!*"

"RAVEN!" Imani exclaimed as a bolt of lightning flashed across the sky. Sudden weather changes in St. Louis didn't faze me or my driving skills. Instead, I braced myself for the thunder. Not from the storm but from *Imani!* "How could you *say* such a thing?!?"

"Because this isn't the first time this has happened to *either* one of us not to mention countless others, both male and female. I mean *REALLY*?!? Is it *that* hard to be faithful to *one* person these days?" I inquired as a roll of thunder echoed over us. It was at least a decibel lower than my sister!

"That doesn't mean you should wish harm on someone," Imani stated as she turned on my car stereo. "Remember what goes around..."

"Comes around," I finished, gently swatting Imani's hand as I turned the radio to Foxy 95.5FM to listen to *The Michael Baisden Show*.

With a raised eyebrow and instantly piqued interest in what my sister was implying, I asked, "So are you saying that *you* cheated on Vincent?"

"No!" Imani blushed as much as a mocha skinned sista could. "I mean that what you put out comes back to you and because I was faithful in my relationships, *including* with Vincent, the Lord will send me the man that's right for me."

Holding back a giggle at Imani's Pollyanna attitude, I couldn't help saying, "But I thought *Vincent* was your 'man sent from God'. Are you telling me you were *supposed* to be cheated on?"

"Raven, you're twisting my words," Imani huffed.

Seeing that I was upsetting my sister, I dropped the subject and instead focused on the radio show. And wouldn't you know that today's topic was about cheating mates!

I still wish a man would dare to cheat on me and think he'll get away with it!

Lightning flashed simultaneously as thunder rolled overhead. Deftly, I navigated the chaotic St. Louis traffic to guide us safely to my favorite *Steak 'n Shake* location.

"It's my own fault," Imani said quietly, looking out of the passenger side window.

I didn't respond until seconds later when we paused at a red light. "How is it *your* fault, Imani? Did *you* make him put that skank between his legs with her head all buried up in his lap?!"

My sister looked at me and rolled her eyes, no doubt at my crass choice of words. "I shouldn't have shown up unannounced."

"Are you fucking kidding me?!?" I shrieked as my anger resurfaced. I nearly peeled out of the intersection the moment the light changed to green.

"Raven! Do you *have* to use profanity?!?" Imani exclaimed in disdain.

"Look, you are only a *few minutes* older than me so quit trying to be Mother!" I snapped back. "And all this hostility you're throwing at me needs to be directed at Vincent's cheatin' ass!"

After a deep breath, Imani apologized. "I know my feelings are misdirected. It's not your fault that Vincent had another woman at his place today. Forgive me?"

Pulling into the *Steak 'n Shake* lot, I accepted my sister's apology. "All I can say is Vincent is damn lucky to have had you because his tires would've been hella flat not to mention he'd have a few busted windows by now if he was *my* man!" I said before humming Jazmine Sullivan's "Bust Your Windows" while pretending to bust the windows on my windshield.

Imani smiled sweetly. "I'll be sure to keep you at the top of my prayer list, Sis."

As we entered the restaurant, you would've thought it was a scene from *Cheers* when the whole bar shouts out "Norm!" except we heard "Raven!" Whenever my office did a lunch run, whoever had the best coupons won and most of those times it was my best friend Monique Clifton with her ever present *Steak 'n Shake* coupons. She and I used the absence from the office not only as an opportunity to get away from our desks, but also to get some midday flirting in. Who knew fry cooks could be so damn sexy!

Moments after Imani and I sat ourselves in my favorite booth, our waitress came to take our orders.

"Welcome to *Steak 'n Shake*. I'm Aisha and I'll be your server this afternoon," she said to Imani.

Looking up from her menu, Imani replied, "I need a few minutes but in the meantime, I'll take a cherry Coke, no ice."

"Sure thing," Aisha said before turning to me. "Your usual, Raven?"

"Put my food order in with hers but I'll take my shake now," I smiled. "Thanks Eesh."

"No prob, Ray," she smiled back.

Looking dumbfounded, Imani watched as Aisha walked away. "She didn't even wait for you to tell her what kind of shake you wanted!"

Chuckling, I stated, "Imani, as much as I eat here, I wouldn't be surprised if they started preparing my meal the minute we walked in and had it finished before we sat down in this booth!"

"Oh!" Imani blushed as Aisha returned with our drinks.

"Ready to order?" Aisha smiled attentively at Imani after placing her drink in front of her.

As my sister ordered her lunch, her cell phone rang. Imani sighed in exasperation after looking at the caller ID display.

"Vincent?" I asked without looking up from my banana mocha side by side shake.

"Yes," she replied flatly. Imani's phone chirped to let her know that she had a voicemail message. "I'm not in the mood to deal with him right now. Ray, since my car is going to be in the shop for another week,

I'll need you to go back with me to get my things."

"Of course, Sis," I said patting her hand.

We ate our late Sunday afternoon lunch and chatted about work, men and our mom, all in between Vincent's phone calls, voicemails and text messages. Eventually, I reached across the table and turned off Imani's phone.

"Raven, what am I doing wrong?" asked my sister as she pushed away her half empty plate.

"The only thing you're doing wrong is thinking that *you* are doing something wrong!" I replied. "Up to this point, has Vincent done or said anything to make you think he would cheat on you?"

"No," Imani said, frowning as she looked out the window just as the sun's rays broke through the grey clouds above.

"So why would he suddenly do this? Knowing you have access to his apartment and can walk in at any moment, why would Vincent cheat on you at his place?" I asked, against my better judgment, considering that *I* had no idea why Vincent would be so foolish!

"I don't really know why, Ray," Imani said turning her gaze toward me. The pain in her eyes made me want to go back to Vincent's and make him hurt as bad as my sister was feeling right now. I tried to keep the rest of our conversation on lighter fare but Imani's thoughts were clearly elsewhere.

In an effort to change the subject, I inquired about my sister's writing.

"Are you still doing spoken word at *Legacy?*" I asked.

"Not lately," Imani half smiled. "With everything being so crazy at work, it's been hard to settle down long enough to write but I keep my notebook and pen nearby at all times."

"Sounds like me," I said as I reached into my purse for my writing essentials: a pen and a mini-notebook. As I flashed them for Imani, I imitated the credit card commercial. "I never leave home without them!"

It was nice to hear my sister's laugh.

~◦~

Later that evening as I prepared for bed, I received a text message from an unexpected source.

BSTJ87: Hey Beautiful. Whatcha doin?

"What the hell?" I said, looking at the cell phone.

BLACKBIRD: Nuthin. Goin 2 bed.

BSTJ87: Can I be your pillow?

Sighing in annoyance, I waited a minute before replying as I thought back to the last time I'd seen Brian St. James. While he seemed to be happy with our Booty Call arrangement, I was at a point in my life where I needed more than the occasional touch of a man and instead desired the security of a stable and faithful relationship. Brian didn't act like he wanted a full time girlfriend so we parted ways.

BLACKBIRD: No time 4 games. U know what I want. U're not ready.

BSTJ87: Who says I'm not?

I couldn't believe I actually got excited from his response!!

BLACKBIRD: Don't play Brian

I'd been messing around with Brian for the past couple of years. Since he didn't act like he wanted a serious relationship, he was the ideal Maintenance Man for me while I was in between boyfriends. Brian was respectful of any situation I was in but no sooner than I'd broken up with my *l'amour du jour*, any time I got that *itch*, Brian was there to scratch it! Eventually, I wanted more than just casual sex and, compared to the ones before him, I knew that Brian was the right man for me. But, being the intelligent sista that I am, I wasn't about to waste my time convincing Brian if *he* wasn't already on the same page!

Been there, done that. Not playing that game anymore just to get hurt again.

BSTJ87: Raven, I need you

"You *need* me?" I said quietly aloud. I got warm shivers from reading those words!!

Could Brian be just as ready as I am to be in a committed relationship?

BSTJ87: You still there?

BLACKBIRD: Yes

BSTJ87: Can I come over tonight?

BLACKBIRD: 2moro's betta

BSTJ87: After work?

BLACKBIRD: Yes

BSTJ87: See you tomorrow Beautiful

Grinning, I slipped into my queen sized bed with thoughts of a real relationship with Brian.

"I wonder if Brian is as good outside the bedroom as he is in it," I said to myself as I settled into bed, preparing to let the TV lull me to sleep as ideas for our first date popped into my brain.

"He said 'Raven I need you'," I said as I re-read our text conversation. Finally, I had hope for Brian and me.

Shaking my head, making my locs swing back and forth, I came back to reality.

Just because he said he needs you doesn't mean he's not talking about sex. That was Randy's line, too, remember?

Damn! It's a good thing my conscience kicked in! I was liable to do the same thing with Brian that I did with my ex-lover, Randy Boorman.

No more half-assed relationships, Raven. Either you're the only woman or you're nobody's woman!

Smiling to myself, I said, "Amen to that!"

Read the full story in…

**Neva Saw It Comin' SistaGirlz Book #3
Raven & Imani's Story**

**E-book available NOW on
www.Leanpub.com**

Excerpt from Her Ideal Husband

SistaGirlz Book #6 Nina's Story

Fun loving and free spirited Nina DeVille was the LAST of the SistaGirlz to WANT to settle down. Hypnotized by the aloofness of her non-committal lover Yusuf Williams, Nina has to decide if "shacking up" is really the way she wants to live her life.

You shouldn't have to drop down to my level. I need to step up to yours and I'm not there yet. I don't know how long it'll take but until then, I can't be with you.

And with that, he was gone.

Sitting there in tears, I replayed that night over and over in my head. Where had we gone wrong? We were having a nice dinner to celebrate our one-year anniversary of living together. Wine was flowing. Music was playing.

Then I suggested that we take a vacation together.

"Baby, you and I need a getaway so I've been looking at vacation packages in the Caribbean," I beamed before taking a bite into Yusuf's mouthwatering roast beef and skin-on red potatoes. The flavors danced on my tongue as I went on and on about all of the fun my boyfriend and I could have in the islands.

"I'll think about it," Yusuf replied quietly as he finished his meal.

"Baby, is everything OK?" I asked with concern. "You sound a little down."

"It's nothing," he stated firmly.

"Baby if something's bothering you, it bothers me," I said as I reached across the table to hold his hand.

"I don't think I should go on vacation right now," Yusuf said plainly.

Waiting for his explanation, I sat and watched Yusuf. When no answer came, I asked, "Why not? Baby, in the year we've lived together, I've never seen you take any personal time off from work. Scheduled days off don't count," I added with a giggle to help lighten the somber mood.

"Look, I just got this job and I don't have the time or money for a vacation!" he snapped, yanking his hand out of mine to grab his glass. Gulping down the last of its contents, I flinched as Yusuf slammed the stemware onto the glass tabletop.

Taken aback by his tone and actions, I replied, "I haven't even said when. As for the money, you know we got it."

"No, *you* have money. I don't," he pointed out as he abruptly rose from the table to take his plate into the kitchen.

Confused by the entire conversation, I followed my boyfriend to get clarification. "Yusuf, what is going on?"

Holding his head down as he stood at the sink, he replied, "Nina, when we met, you had everything I dreamed of. A nice home. A working vehicle. A stable job. I didn't have none of that but when you asked me out, I wasn't gonna say no!" Turning around to face me, he continued, "I figga'd if nuthin else, I'd take you out and show you what I'm capable of. I wasn't gonna tell you that I'd just lost my job, my ride was on its last legs and I was sleepin' on my boy's couch."

"Well, no, I wouldn't expect you to tell me that on our first date but did I leave when you told me?" I asked as I walked over and hugged him. Laying my head on his chest, I smiled nervously as I listened to his rapid heartbeat.

I wonder if his heart was beating this fast that night I asked him out. I just wanted someone to hang out with and since we were both in *Oscar's* playing pool alone every Friday night, why not get to know if there's more to this cutie other than his fine ass is *almost* as good a pool player as I am?

"Then three months of dating later you ask me to move in with you," Yusuf continued. "I said no and you threw a fit."

"Hey!" Laughing as I stood at arm's length away from my man, I said, "That wasn't a fit. I simply pointed out that you had no good reason to say no! You mean you would rather sleep on that lumpy smelly ass couch at Victor's place?"

"Yes!" he laughed back.

"Wait... What?!?" I snapped. "Hold up, Yusuf. What are you saying?"

"Listen," he said firmly adding a look to let me know I needed to stay silent. I hated when he did that but I couldn't get any answers until

I stopped asking questions. Calmly, he said, "I said no because we were just dating and still getting to know each other. If you needed help with anything, I was a phone call away."

He's right. He didn't have to drive back and forth in that hooptie when he could have just as easily stayed overnight after "getting to know me". I lived closer to his job and he knew he could drop me off on his way to work. But he eventually saw my side and moved in.

"On the night we celebrate our one year anniversary of living together, you telling me you'd rather live elsewhere isn't going to go over well. You do realize this?" I said coolly.

His crooked smile was his attempt to let me know that he was wrong for that. "Dammit Nina!!" he laughed, mimicking Martin Lawrence's famous line from his self-titled sitcom. "My point is we both need a vacation but I'm just getting on my feet and I don't want to hold you up if you trynna do this anytime soon."

"I wasn't thinking anytime soon because I wanted you to help me plan our vacation," I said, pulling closer to him, nudging him against the kitchen counter. "As for the money, if you want to do it 50/50, that's fine. We can figure out who pays for what later. We don't have to do it tonight."

"I don't know when I'll be able to take a vacation, Nina," Yusuf replied with a hard tone.

Not wanting to turn this into a shouting match, I replied, "OK, Baby."

As Yusuf proceeded to clear the dining room table and start the dishes, I retreated to our master bedroom to retrieve his gift from our walk-in closet. Walking back toward the living room, I found my sexy boyfriend lounging on the leather sofa with the TV tuned to a sports show.

As many times as Yusuf has tried to get me to sit down and watch a game with him, they all looked alike to me. I couldn't tell you the difference between a touchdown, a home run or a triple-double. I only know a sports star if they end up on the news. I'm not talking during the allotted sports segment but instead because of some hook up with a non-sports celebrity. Other than running into them at various nightlife events, I didn't even know any sports players to root for!

Before interrupting his viewing, I watched the widescreen television long enough to discern that my Baby was catching up on the highlights of tonight's NBA Finals game. If I wanted to root for his team with him, the least I could do was see what the score was. Never hurts to do a little homework. If his team was winning, I was almost assured our evening would go well into the night. If his boys were losing, I would be prepared to console him.

Slowly, I brought Yusuf's gift from behind my back and sat it on his lap.

"Babe, what's this?" he said, looking up at me in confusion. "I thought we agreed we weren't doing gifts."

"I thought you were kidding!" I replied in genuine surprise. "I mean you made your melt-in-my-mouth roast beef and skin-on red potatoes. You only do that on special occasions!"

"Yeah, you wanted to celebrate and I knew you wanted me to cook that tonight with all of the hints you dropped this week," Yusuf pointed out.

"Oh… well, actually this is a gift for the both of us," I smiled sheepishly. "Happy Anniversary!"

I held my breath as Yusuf slowly opened the gift-wrapped box containing a large manila envelope. As he pulled the documents from the envelope, I said, "You don't have to sign it now.

Go over it, check the spelling, ask questions. I just couldn't wait another day to give it to you!"

Yusuf quickly flipped through the pages. "It looks like your condo lease with my name added to it."

Dumbfounded that he wasn't as excited as I was, I said, "Yeah, remember when you moved in and said that if we're still together after a year, you'll make this permanent?"

"Whoa!!" he cried out as he leapt off the couch. "Are you proposing to me?!?"

Stifling my laughter, I replied, "Did a ring fall out of that envelope? No. I'm just asking you to move in permanently. You moved all of your stuff in, didn't you?"

"Nina…" Yusuf slipped the lease back into the envelope. "I didn't have that much to begin with. Most of what's in my closet came from you."

"You say that like it's a bad thing," I frowned, unsure where this conversation was heading.

Walking over to me, Yusuf held me in his arms. "Practically everything I have is because of you. My home. My job. My car."

Looking up at him, I said, "I did all of that because I love you and want you to be happy."

"And I thank you for everything but I can't do any of that for you," he replied. "This is your home that you asked me to move into. I'm driving because you loaned me one of your cars. The job I have is because my boss is a friend of yours."

"And the problem is?" I asked in exasperation.

"If you lost your job, I couldn't support us. Hell, I'm still trynna catch my breath from all of the shit I got into before I met you!"

"Baby, I told you I can help you with that," I offered again, sensing Yusuf's tension increasing. "And if I lost my job, my savings and investments could support us until I found something else. You know I wouldn't have a problem with that."

"Nina, stop! Just stop!!" Yusuf pulled himself out of our embrace. "You can't fix all of my problems!! Some of this doesn't even concern you! I'm not gonna let you pay for my mistakes!"

"OK, fine! Sorry I offered but that's no reason to yell at me!" I snapped back.

"A raised voice is not the same as yelling, Nina," Yusuf stated in a more gentle tone. "No matter how I try to explain it, you just don't get it!"

"So what are you saying, Yusuf?" I asked nervously, not emotionally prepared for his response as I followed him to the front door.

Sighing as he opened the door, he said, "You shouldn't have to drop down to my level. I need to step up to yours and I'm not there yet. I don't know how long it'll take but until then, I can't be with you."

One of the things I loved about Yusuf was that he usually said exactly what he meant and had I been listening the first time, I would've heard him say that although he wants to be, he's not where I am in life. But I didn't care that he didn't have my money or possessions or that he couldn't get them for me. I loved Yusuf just the way he was!

The next day when I returned home from meeting up with my girls for our weekly Sunday Brunch, I found my condo not as I'd left it. None of Yusuf's belongings were where I'd last seen them. His Jordans weren't cluttering up the doorway from me tossing them out of his closet. The hallway was clear of his clothes that I'd flung out of the bedroom hamper. His closet was empty of everything he'd moved in with. Only the clothes I bought him were on the hangers.

Quickly, I dialed Yusuf's cell phone number. Growing impatient as each ring went unanswered, I visually searched my residence of any sign of my lover but nothing was to be found.

"The person you have called is unavailable right now. Please try again later."

Read the full story in...

Her Ideal Husband SistaGirlz Book #6

BUY THIS E-BOOK NOW, GET THE
UPDATES FOR FREE!!!!

Excerpt from Clarissa's Trilogy

SistaGirlz Book #8

Clarissa Revelin lives life by her own rules and she'll cut you off of her lovin' QUICK if you break them! Even her long-time lover Franklin Gilbert has a hard time pinning her down for long! Never one to fall for just anything anyone tells her, Clarissa is the freest spirit of all of the SistaGirlz!!

CLARISSA & FRANKLIN

CLARISSA

FRANK84: "Baby are you still mad at me?"
Ignoring Franklin's texts, I occupied my time by cleaning the condo. Per my lover's request, Franklin's mother stopped by to work

on her project while keeping tabs on me while Franklin was at work. The extra bedroom was officially off limits while Mama Gilbert prepared to turn it into Olivia's nursery.

"Baby, is everything alright?" Mama Gilbert asked when I swept the same kitchen corner for the third time in a row.

"Huh? Oh! Well… It's something I need to discuss with Franklin but we've had this discussion before and I don't know if I can follow through on the solution in my condition," I stated as I put my cleaning supplies away.

"And that was clear as mud, Baby. What's going on with you and Franklin?" Mama Gilbert asked.

"His jealousy is too much for me to handle right now, Mama!" I began. "Yesterday when you called and I told you I wasn't feeling well, he started freaking out because he thought you were gonna come over and take care of me. Since yesterday was his last day off before going back to work, he wanted me all to himself."

"Well, I can understand that but what's got you so worked up about that?" she asked.

"A few minutes after you called me, the doorbell rang. Immediately Franklin went ballistic! I had to remind him that it could be you at the door but instead it was my ex-boyfriend Mackenzie!" I explained.

"The idiot that cheated on you before you went back to Franklin?" she asked.

"Yes ma'am," I replied. "He came over to work things out but I still don't know how he got our address in the first place!"

"There's nothing to work out! You both cheated on each other. What kind of foundation is that for a relationship?" Mama Gilbert asked sincerely.

"Not a very sturdy one, that's for sure!" I frowned. "Mama, why is he doing this to me? Hasn't he hurt me enough by cheating on me?!"

"He didn't make the decision to end your relationship so he believes there's still a chance at reconciliation," Mama Gilbert explained. "Talk to him with Franklin. Maybe once he sees how happy you are without him, if he loves you, he'll let you be happy with Franklin."

"Mackenzie chose to end our relationship when he fucked Sabrina," I thought to myself.

"I hope so," I said as I received another apology text from Franklin. I replied: "We need to talk."

As expected, I didn't get a text. I got a phone call.

"Sexy, I love you and I'm sorry," Franklin apologized. "That wasn't jealousy. I was pissed cuz he caught me off guard! How in the hell did he know where we lived?!"

"Baby, I don't know since I've always been unlisted and I never told him your name," I admitted. "But that doesn't explain why you hit him."

"Sexy, you heard the message I left him. And he wouldn't leave when you told him to!" Franklin said in his defense.

"But to punch him?! You didn't even TRY to talk to him, Franklin!" I said angrily, prompting Mama Gilbert to shoot a stern look in my direction. Getting up from the sofa to get myself a glass of egg nog (minus my favorite shot of Sailor Jerry rum), I continued. "I feel trapped in this situation, Franklin. Normally I leave you alone for a few days when you do this but I have nowhere to go!"

"Baby! No, no, no, no, no!! Don't leave me! I'm sorry I lost my temper! Please don't leave me!" Franklin begged.

Losing my anger at my lover, I said, "You're lucky my stomach isn't fully settled or else I wouldn't've stuck around to hear your pathetic begging," I laughed.

"Get any phone calls?" he inquired, still sounding nervous.

"Just this one from you," I said truthfully.

"Are you in the living room or the bedroom?" Franklin asked, finally sounding relieved.

"In the kitchen headed back into the living room," I smiled at Baby Daddy's concern. "I was just getting a drink."

"Is Ma there?" he inquired.

"Yeah. She's in the nursery," I said as I planted my booty in the middle of the sofa.

"Lemme talk to her, please?" Franklin couldn't hide his tactics. If he wanted to know how I was, why wasn't *my* word enough?!

"Hold on," I sighed. Before I could get one foot on the floor, Mama Gilbert came out of the nursery. "Mama, Franklin wants to talk to you."

"Thank you, Baby. Go and lay down. You've had enough excitement for one day!" Mama Gilbert urged as I headed for my bedroom.

FRANKLIN

"Ma, has she gotten any phone calls?" I

asked, fearful that Clarissa had been getting harassed by Mackenzie on my first day away from her.

"Just this one from you," Ma said, confirming what Clarissa told me. It's not that I didn't want to believe her but knowing Clarissa, she wouldn't want to upset me by telling me that Mackenzie had called or stopped by while I was gone. Having Ma at the house helped ease my mind as I hoped it would cut down on the chance of an ex sighting.

"Maybe Sexy and I should think about moving into a new spot after we…" I thought to myself.

"Ma, how much have you done on the extra bedroom?" I asked, struggling to contain my excitement.

"Measured the walls and shopped online with Clarissa for furniture. Why?" Ma asked, being nosey.

"Just asking. Tell Clarissa I'll call her later. Love you, Ma," I smiled as I hung up before taking a peek at the box in my desk drawer

By the end of my workday, I was so hyped about what I was about to say to Clarissa that I could've floated home! When I arrived home, I found Clarissa in the kitchen, preparing dinner.

Even with her back to me, I knew she was still pissed about me hitting Mackenzie so I came home with a peace offering: a bouquet of roses.

Reaching around her to put the flowers in her hands, I said, "Sexy, I'm sorry."

"You've already apologized, Franklin. Just don't let it happen again," she said, laying the flowers on the sink counter without looking at me.

Turning her to face me, I said, "I've been doing some thinking and I was wondering how would you feel about moving into a new house."

Looking up at me, Clarissa exclaimed, "What?! Why??"

"I want our daughter to have a room of her own in the house she'll grow up in and the condo isn't big enough." Kneeling on one knee, I continued. "And I want to pick that house with her mother. Clarissa Olivia Revelin, will you marry me?"

"Franklin... I... I..."

Before I knew it, Clarissa passed out! Catching her before her head hit the floor, I gently shook and kissed her as we sat on the kitchen floor. I called Clarissa's name until she responded. "Sexy, wake up! Wake up Clarissa!"

Slowly coming to, Clarissa's eyes fluttered as she looked up at me.

"Baby, you fainted," I said with a sigh of relief that Clarissa was conscious.

"Did you just ask me to marry you?!" Clarissa asked in disbelief.

"Yes, Sexy. What do you say?" I smiled.

What she said next wasn't the response I expected to receive.

Looking up at me with tears in her eyes, Clarissa said, "Franklin, there's something I need to tell you."

Read the full story in…

Clarissa's Trilogy SistaGirlz Book #8

Part 1 - Her Last Seven Deadly Sinful Days
Part 2 - She's A Hard Habit To Break
Part 3 - Her Last First Kiss

BUY THIS E-BOOK NOW, GET THE UPDATES FOR FREE!!!!

The Books of Author Lea Mishell

Paperbacks are coming soon. All of my
e-books are available at
https://leanpub.com/u/LeaMishell

*BUY THESE E-BOOKS NOW, GET THE
UPDATES FOR FREE!!!!*

Author Lea Mishell Pricing

(Effective September 16, 2021)

**E-books available NOW on (or COMING
SOON to) Leanpub**

**Livin' Just Enough SistaGirlz Book #1
Rachael's Story** *(What He Did For Her Love
Edition)*

Illusions SistaGirlz Book #2 Layla's Story

**Neva Saw It Comin' SistaGirlz Book #3
Raven & Imani's Story**

**Unexpected Detours SistaGirlz Book #4
Meeka's Story**

**Unforgivable SistaGirlz Book #5 Angela's
Story**

**Her Ideal Husband SistaGirlz Book #6
Nina's Story**

JaShel's Trilogy SistaGirlz Book #7

Clarissa's Trilogy SistaGirlz Book #8

SistaGirlz Finale...? SistaGirlz Book #9

You Me Him Her Mistress Harding Book 1

SistaGirlz Monogamy Package

All of the monogamous **SistaGirlz** stories

SistaGirlz Polyamory Package

All of the polyamorous **SistaGirlz** stories

SistaGirlz Ethical Non-Monogamy Package

All of the ethically non-monogamous **SistaGirlz** stories

The SistaGirlz Collection

Get ALL of my **SistaGirlz** e-books in one bundle!

The Lea Mishell Part 1 Collection

The Lea Mishell Collection is a digital library of every book I will ever write. **The**

Lea Mishell Collection Part 1 is available on
Leanpub at
https://leanpub.com/b/TheLeaMishellCollection-
Part-1. As of October 1, 2021, I will add the
second part.

Happy Reading!!!

PeaceLoveHappinessPolyamory
Lm…